Mi

for

Murder

by
Rosie Lear

Grosvenor House
Publishing Limited

This book is published by
Grosvenor House Publishing Ltd
Link House
140 The Broadway, Tolworth, Surrey, KT6 7HT.
www.grosvenorhousepublishing.co.uk

This book is a work of fiction but based upon real-life historical events
and characters. The story is a product of the author's imagination and
should not be construed as true.

A CIP record for this book
is available from the British Library

ISBN 978-1-78623-267-0

Dedicated to the memory of my husband, Alan,
without whose love and support this would
never have been written.
He did not live to see the publication, but certainly
lived patiently through the birth of this first gentle
adventure into medieval murder.

Chapter 1

Cheap Street was silent in the glistening moonlight, roofs shining unevenly, their windows dark and silent under frozen eaves. A cold wind blew as Thomas Copeland lifted the latch of his house. He paused at the threshold, glad to smell the familiar sweet and fragrant rushes which carpeted his floors. His maidservant Hannah had expected his return today and had renewed them in anticipation of his homecoming.

Thomas breathed in deeply, satisfied with his day's work. He had dined well with a former pupil of his, one Matthias Barton, who lived in the nearby village of Milborne Port. His horse was safely stabled after his ride home – some four miles, and Thomas, no longer a young man, was pleasantly tired. He had known and liked the Barton family for many years and had been much saddened when the family was decimated by sweating sickness, leaving only Matthias, then just sixteen years of age.

Now he had been pleased to welcome Matthias back to the family home, and to advise him on his plans to open a small school for a few boys, using his family home as a base. Matthias, he knew, had some private income and a suitably large house near the church, and was a patient young man, sufficiently able to build up his proposed small group of boys who lived too far from Sherborne to benefit from Thomas' own school.

For Thomas Copeland was himself a teacher, engaged by the monks of Sherborne Abbey to instruct the scholars who looked to the Abbey for education.

The Abbey stood slightly down hill from where he stood, awesome and solid, and with more building work going on. Within its walls the monks sung their offices eight times daily, and went about their work of prayer and obedience – although obedient these days to a more pampered regime than in his father's time, Thomas thought ruefully, as he closed the door on the silent street.

He rubbed his hand over his tired face as he prepared to retire. He was a slightly built man, his back beginning to stoop, brown hair now streaked with silver and his eyes, somewhat sore after his recent ride in the wind and the gathering dusk took in with appreciation the work Hannah had done today. He laid his travelling cloak carefully over the carved wooden chair and loosened his boots, wincing at the mild back pain caused by his ride home.

He had left Matthias' house rather late, so the last mile of his journey had been in semi-darkness – not a safe or sensible thing for a man of his age for despite the simplicity of his attire, the quality of his clothes spoke of a man who enjoyed and could afford quality.

Thomas' door was closed, as another shadowy door opened cautiously further down. The dark, enveloping cloak and cowl admitted no clue as to the identity of the owner. Swiftly towards the darkened Abbey the figure went, without looking behind or to the side, and keeping carefully to the shadows. It was a black night despite a weak moon, the cobbled streets deserted. At the corner of the Shambles the figure paused to wait for another such hooded figure to join him; neither hood nor cowl fell back to reveal their faces as the two passed without word through the gate and into the Abbey grounds. Night swallowed them. An evil little breeze marked their passing.

Abbot Bradford stirred restlessly, his knees troubling him as he knelt at prayer. His woven linen nightshift was open at the neck, for he was ready to retire, but he was unable to compose his mind sufficiently to concentrate on his office. The bitter quarrel with Father Samuel, priest of All Hallows, threatened to escalate out of all proportion and bit into his mind.

All Hallows joined the Abbey and was where the common townspeople worshipped. Father Samuel, their priest, was a champion of the people, unafraid to speak out, fierce in his condemnation of the Abbot's regime. His pale grey eyes had blazed in his thin aesthetic face as he had faced Abbot Bradford on the Abbey Green, spittle landing on the Abbot's cloak. The quarrel today had been decidedly unchristian and extremely public. He, Abbot Bradford, had felt fully justified for the things he had said. The townspeople WERE noisy and common...oh, Father Samuel had accused him of snobbery and a lack of compassion for that . . . how *dare* he . . . and the *demands* of the people had been thrust under his aristocratic nose . . . they had no right to DEMAND anything of him . . he was The Abbot. He *would* be respected.

The flavour of the argument crept into his prayers . . . there had been undignified name calling, denials concerning the rights of the townspeople . . . accusations of hypocrisy and self indulgence (some of which, if he was totally honest, he should have agreed with) but he felt totally justified in his actions – there was no doubt in his mind that the doorway between the Abbey and neighbouring All Hallows *should* have been narrowed. It gave for a more disciplined walk during processionals, and it gave the common and often noisy townspeople less opportunity to spy shamelessly on the brothers as they sung their daily offices. If the truth be known, there were often less monks than there should have been singing, for laziness and self indulgence had crept in to the monastic life. Sherborne was a rich jewel in the Bishop's mitre, and as Abbot, he knew his share of the pickings could be worthwhile . . . but the decidedly unchristian quarrel he now had with Father Samuel was eating at his very soul. *He* was the Abbot – his word *would* be respected. The unseemly and undignified encounter with Samuel that day had left him filled with righteous anger and indignation.

He had already appealed to Bishop Neville of Salisbury in an effort to end this pettiness. The resulting enquiry of some months previously had been attended by some hundred townspeople and had been a noisy affair. Bishop Neville had wisely tried to support aspects of both sides, but his orders had not been carried out by either party. The font the rebel townsmen had erected in the Chapel of Ease was still there – and no, he would not widen the doorway until they removed the font. He would appeal to Bishop Neville again if necessary.

He quivered with anger, even while on his knees in attempted prayer. His great work was the continuation of the rebuilding of parts of the Abbey, a magnificent architectural work of which he was very proud. It was his passion to complete the work started by his predecessor, Abbot Brunyng, and his drive and enthusiasm obliterated every other thought in his head. This humiliating and pernicious quarrel poisoned his thoughts and he could not rest . . . even found it difficult to pray.

He moved to end his vigil. His well-fleshed knees ached and cracked, and he eased his back with the flat of his hand as he rose to his feet.

Abbot Bradford was a tall, heavily built man running to fat; proud and haughty towards his fellow men, his face bore signs of rich living. His nose was the most prominent feature in his face, and he used it to good effect often to look down disparagingly at those he considered beneath him. His elevated position as Abbot over twenty four monks, seven infirmarians and their retinue of lay workers gave him a somewhat inflated sense of his position. He was feared by his brothers and openly disliked by the good townspeople. Their enthusiastic applause of Father Samuel during the public acrimonious exchange that afternoon concerning the door in the Abbey had enraged him rather than shaken him. His plump cheeks flamed afresh as he remembered the scene – twenty angry tradesmen, ranging from silversmiths, fletchers, cloth merchants, glovers through to several women and a crowd of masons and their apprentices, listening avidly as Father Samuel championed their cause, berating the Abbot for being high-handed, lacking sympathy, failing to show humility – oh, it went on and on . . . . and all that from a man whose grasp of the required Latin was so slight . . . a man so far beneath him in learning and breeding . . a mere priest in charge . . . unlettered and without land . . . but fired with tremendous passion for the perceived rights and needs of his flock . . .

Abbot Bradford shook his head angrily – *He* would decide how the Abbey was to be run – he would not be dictated to by such a man – hadn't he taken over the visionary new building started by his predecessor, Abbot Brunyng? Didn't that make him every bit a man of vision as Abbot Brunyng had been so described? How *dare* Father Samuel question his motives.

Quivering with emotion, he moved away from the glassed windows of the house recently built for him – and by so doing, missed the two cowled figures slipping noiselessly through the Abbey garden

Brother Francis found sleep difficult. He had partaken of too much good wine and roast meats, a welcome change from the unending diet of fish, for this was the season of Lenten fare. The Abbey refectory was too well provided for these days... gone were the days of his novitiate, when poverty and abstinence were observed more closely and absence at the divine offices was rewarded by penance . . . he had seen some radical changes in monastic life, and now as an old man, he had allowed himself to be content with the slackness, regarding it as progress rather than regression. The monks of Sherborne lived well.

He stumbled from his bed to ease his digestion with a short walk. Quietly, for fear of waking his fellow brothers in the long dortoir, he moved to the glassless window which overlooked the garden. Opposite was the Abbot's new house, solidly built of Purbeck stone and offering a degree of privacy hitherto unknown. Brother Francis jumped slightly as a tree appeared to move. As he watched, the tree became a cloaked figure moving towards the Abbey. The figure turned into two, silently gliding in the moonlit darkness of this chilly March night before disappearing from view against the shadowy walls. Brother Francis shook his head – he was old; the monastic life had become pampered – who was he to tell tales if his fellow brothers slipped out to whore's alley now and again? It did not occur to him to count the sleeping forms behind him in the dortoir, or to see whether there were any empty beds. He returned to his own bed, and fell asleep instantly.

The heavy doors of the Abbey swung open without sound as the cloaked figures reached it. The great grey stones of the floor were marked with the residue of dust from the building work – the fine dust they created flew everywhere. Bare feet made no noise on the cold stone floor, although in the dust, slight footprints were left. The moon which had dangerously lit their progress slid behind a cloud, hiding the hard glitter of their concealed daggers. Pressed close to the soaring pillars, their progress down the great nave was slow and cautious, dodging the detritus of the day's labour, for the workmen had appropriated the nave as their yard, and part of the great building was open to the sky, pending temporary shelter of thatch until the new work could be completed.

Surprise was their best weapon – daggers only their second. They held their breath, the better to surprise their quarry. He had become too greedy; his threats of exposure to the Abbot had sealed his fate – he had to die. They passed seamlessly into the Lady Chapel, no more than dark shadows on the soul, killing machines to the core. The young man waited patiently for them expecting his new instructions, and his increased reward. His soft shoes had made little sound when he'd entered; his short dark green cotte and brown hose indicated a man of some skill – a craftsman. He was nervous, but also elated, for his baseless threats to these strangers appeared to have been successful. They had indeed promised increased reward. He thought briefly of his young wife and the child expected so soon – how fine it would be to indulge her in some luxuries for herself and the new child. He was unaware that it would be his last thought.

His task for them was incomplete. He had been promised simplicity, and suddenly it had become more sinister and considerably more difficult. He needed more coins, over and above those already given to him . . . and stage payment for his discoveries, or, he had told them, he would have to speak to the Abbot. As a mere apprentice his access to the Abbot was far removed, but he had innocently hoped the idle threat would bring him success so there could be an end to this affair. He had sorely miscalculated his adversaries, for he was a simple country young man, unused to complicated plots and double dealings. What had seemed a useful way of earning extra coin had suddenly become more serious, but he was determined to hold his nerve, and so he was doing exactly as he had been told, confident that his nerve would bring the expected reward.

The chill of the Abbey was penetrating his bones – he was kneeling as he had always been instructed – facing the altar – and although his ear was pricked for the sound of his task-masters, he heard no sound behind him . . . only a sudden raising of the hairs on the back of his neck before the first dagger found its mark, sliding in to soft tissue as easily as a knife to butter . . . a choked strangled gurgle . . . a gush of warm, sticky blood flooding the stones beneath his collapsing knees . . . a second dagger thrust, more accurate than the first . . . strong cruel hands covering his mouth . . . pressing into his neck . . . he jerked in death spasm . . . tried to turn to see his attacker . . . failed . . . a rasp of breath sprayed fountains of blood over his tunic . . .

Gouts of blood stained the floor and ran into the cracks between the grey flag stones as the shadowy figures wiped their blood encrusted daggers on his tunic before retreating as swiftly and silently as they'd come, silent killers who knew their business well.

Chapter 2

Matthias Barton's plans for a simple scholastic establishment in his home were well advanced. He had spoken long and carefully with his one-time schoolmaster and now friend, Thomas Copeland, and he admired his organization, sense of purpose and discipline. Thomas' school was ordered by the Sherborne monks, who wished suitable boys to be educated with a view to entering the church or the law. Thomas Copeland taught them grammar, astronomy, logic, arithmetic and geometry, following the liberal arts programme of the two great universities. His pupils were mostly the sons of wealthy families or prosperous merchants, some of whom might aspire to the new universities in distant Oxford and Cambridge. Thomas Copeland himself was an Oxford scholar and valued learning as the path to progress. He had met a variety of men at Oxford who had different aspirations - some even now had achieved high office in the service of the King, but Thomas had been content to return to Sherborne and take up the position as schoolmaster, that others might satisfy their quest for learning.

His time at Oxford had not been entirely happy - he was always cold, always poor, his lodgings were inadequate and shared with four other students as impecunious as himself, - and the plague had retreated only a few years before, leaving an unhealthy atmosphere of fear and apprehension among the decimated population.

Here in Sherborne, he lived his life with his work amongst the scholars, such as they were. Hannah, his maidservant, looked after his every need and he had earned a degree of respect from the townspeople as well as from the Abbot. His young wife had died in child-birth in 1400, the child with her, and he had never sought the company of women again, preferring instead to bury himself in his work. There were very few such schools as his - many were still attached to the abbeys and monasteries of the land and accepted only such young boys as had been encouraged to enter orders, either by choice or because they were second or third sons of less wealthy gentry. He was fortunate that the easy-going and lax rules of Sherborne encouraged the monks to seek to relinquish the arduous task of instructing the young.

Matthias Barton had been a pupil of his twelve years ago, - a ready and willing lad, eager to learn, serious by nature and utterly devoted to his two sisters, to whom he would impart all the knowledge he gained from Master Copeland. Matthias' grandfather had seen service as a soldier in France under King Henry V and for his services had been granted land in Milborne Port. He had died as Alexander Barton, his son, had completed the building of Barton Holding on the land granted by King Henry, when Matthias was twelve years old.

Seeking to send Matthias to Oxford to study law, Alexander had sold some of the land surrounding Barton Holding to pay the high fees required, - land which had once been farmed by the Bishop of Salisbury's men but had been granted to him in addition to the land already inherited from his father, in gratitude by the King for faithful service during the terrible wars with

France. Father and son – Matthias' father and grandfather, had both served in the great struggle with France, but Matthias had no desire to follow their lead. The intrigue, politics and destruction of war held no appeal for him, and since the Maid Joan had intervened, England was fast losing ground . The young king had not the same stomach for victory as his father and grandfather, and the forces remaining in Normandy were led by young Richard, Duke of York.

His long years at Oxford nearly finished, Matthias returned home distraught on the death of his father from sweating sickness only to be there in time to find his mother and two sisters dying from the same deadly peril.

So aged just twenty and not completely finished with his studies, he abandoned all his hopes and dreams in despair and grief. He left England and traveled the continent, careless of the handsome house he had inherited.

His grief dulled somewhat after four years, he returned to put his life together again... England was a changing place..... he had studied law but was not a lawyer. However, he had the ability and the temperament to instill in others a degree of learning. Indeed, he had done just that for a year, with the Benedictine monks in a small Italian monastery....ragged street boys who came to the good monks for food and who stayed to listen to Matthias' faltering efforts at teaching them.

On his return to Milborne Port, he took advice from Thomas Copeland, despite the fact that Thomas was well past middle-age now. Thomas became his friend and mentor, and now Matthias was ready to begin again.

Barton Holding was a substantially built dwelling, the front door opening into a large hall which would serve as the main room for his scholars. Leading off the hall were two further rooms, one of which was Matthias' personal study and main relaxing place. This had a small ladder leading upwards into a private solar and sleeping place. The other door led into the kitchen with a fire place used for cooking, and a further small room where Davy and his wife Elizabeth slept.

Davy and his wife had kept house for Matthias since he had returned to Milborne Port. The old feudal system of serf and villein was changing fast. Many of Davy's generation were enjoying a new way of life - working for an overlord for monetary gain instead of being bound to his land in exchange for a place to live. Davy's father had been a miller until his death, when the mill had passed to Davy's older brother, Tobias. Tobias and his wife had no need of Davy's services, preferring instead to use the cottagers, whom they could order more as they pleased, and Davy's character was too independent to be always under Tobias' thumb.

Today, a crisp March day with the promise of sun, Matthias sought out Davy to prepare his schoolroom. He found Davy outside in the small courtyard, his square jaw set in unusual lines of concentration as he clipped at the box hedge surrounding the lavender bushes which Matthias' mother had planted.

"Will you be long finishing the clipping, Davy? I think it's time we prepared the tables for the schoolroom."

Davy looked up. "I can finish this later if you wish to start now, Master."

"Finish the clipping and then join me. I can start the tables alone."

Matthias found several trestle boards in his outside store and began to carry them into the yard. They needed scrubbing down before taking them in to his house. He glanced at Davy several times as he worked. Davy's mind was clearly not on his task. He put down the tools and wiped his forehead in perplexity. His expression was clouded, and once or twice he made as if to speak to Matthias and checked himself.

Matthias leaned on one of the trestles, dusting cobwebs from it with his hand.

"Something you want to say to me, Davy?"

Davy's grateful look eased his way.

" Do you remember Ben Glover, Master?"

"I do indeed, Davy – your helpmate in poaching when you were lads! The chief apple scrumper! Weren't you part of his marriage feast last year?'

"That I was, Master....it was just after Elizabeth and I wed...all part of the village, as it should be! Ben's wife, Lydia called on me today. Ben went to Sherborne two days ago and hasn't returned. Lydia asked me to walk out on the track to see if he lies injured. You hear of lawless bands on some trackways. Ben had nothing of value - and looked nothing...." He tailed off, his imagination failing him.

There were no reports of which Matthias knew concerning gangs of outlaws locally, but he supposed it was always possible. The declining and failing war in France had given rise to dispirited soldiers returning whenever they could...rumour was rife that they had not been paid for months, so those that reached England were starving and penniless...and the young king had not the spirit or belly for war that his father had displayed....it was becoming a cause for concern, even in country

districts where news traveled slowly and was often con-
voluted before it reached them

"When did Ben come home, Davy?" he asked.

"A couple of days ago, Master," replied Davy, "He'd
arranged to come especially to be with Lydia for the
birth."

"So why did he suddenly go back to Sherborne?"
wondered Matthias.

Davy shook his head. He had wondered exactly the
same himself, when he'd seen Ben set out, almost furtively, two days ago.

There had been something almost dishonest about
the disappearing figure of his young friend in the afternoon light, - Davy couldn't quite put it into words.

"I hope he hasn't fallen foul of Master Cope,"
Matthias muttered, acidly. "Ben was given special dis-
pensation to come home – the glover won't think too
highly of him if he meets him in the market when he
thinks he's at home."

Davy said nothing – he rubbed one foot awkwardly
against the calf of his other leg, waiting for Matthias to
decide.

"We'll carry these trestles in and set them up, then go
down to Sherborne - take my horse - but do please be
back before sunset."

Davy heaved the trestles onto his shoulders and
edged them through the heavy oak door.

In his heart he was afraid of what he might find –
Ben had altered subtly during the last few months

Once, although he had told no-one, Davy had found
him insensibly drunk in the grounds of the Abbey itself.
As lads together, they had often been drinking partners
when they'd had a few coins to spare, but never had

Davy seen anyone as drunk as Ben had been that night, and in the Abbey...what on earth was he doing on Abbey ground? Davy could find no answer to that.

He was grateful to his master for permission to do Lydia's bidding, and especially grateful for the use of his horse.. Normally if out and about on Matthias' work, Davy would use the nag - quite adequate, but Matthias' horse was a faster, smoother ride.

His friendship with Ben was long standing. They had gleaned corn together after harvest as young boys, had collected stones from the manor field before planting, had shared food when harvests had failed, as had happened several times....bad times they were....this year wasn't going to be too good so folk predicted...fished, poached, joined with villagers in funeral wakes, weddings, just the normal things one did in life. So where was Ben now?

As he neared Pinford, he looked towards Sherborne, half hidden in the fold of the hills. So far there had been no trace of Ben - no signs of a scuffle - no discarded shoes.. no broken bushes... A feeling of deep unease overtook him as he resumed his lonely journey.

The track widened; he passed Pig Hill on his left and jogged wearily down Coldharbour, with its squat houses and higgeldy lanes...still no sign of Ben.

He entered Hound Street Tithing and came into Lodborne Lane, where Ben's lodgings were. He paused on the narrow cobbles and looked anxiously down the alleyway for any sighting of Ben or the maidservant of the house. There were people about, but no sign of Ben.

Children were playing in the leat of water that ran down the centre of the cobbles. It didn't look too clean but with their bare feet they were shouting with glee as they splashed each other with the water. Davy stepped over the stream, designed to carry away night refuse and dismounting, knocked on the door with his knuckles. There was a significant pause before Mistress Fosse, the widow-woman, opened it herself, cautiously. Davy could hear weeping from inside the open hallway. He lowered his eyes respectfully.

"May I see Ben Glover?" he asked.

"Who asks for him?" she replied, falteringly.

"Davy - I'm sent by his wife, Lydia. She is missing him from home."

Mistress Fosse covered her face with her hands and steadied herself on the doorpost.

"His wife? No message has come to her yet? You'd best come in, I cannot talk on the doorsill."

Davy showed a small coin to the oldest of the playing children, who were looking at the scene curiously. If the horse was safe when Davy came out, the child had earned the coin.

Mistress Fosse beckoned Davy into the darkened hallway. The house was a small town house, with one large hall downstairs and an outside kitchen at the back. Upstairs was her small solar, and the room she let to Ben. The serving girl lived in the kitchen and was glad of her position.

The windows were small and covered with parchment, making it hard for Davy to see anything in the hall very clearly.

Mistress Fosse stood looking at him for a moment. She drew breath to speak - thought better of it and covered her face again.

"What is it?" Davy cried, cold suddenly to his heart.

"Ben is dead." Mistress Fosse declared, flatly,

"His body was found this morning lying in the Lady Chapel of the Abbey".

Davy stared at her, the chill in his heart now icy. The murky hall seemed to sway around him.

"No, - there must be some mistake" he exclaimed, "The Lady Chapel? What would he be doing there? He came to Sherborne to deliver something."

Mistress Fosse shivered violently, despite the fire burning in her central hearth.

"He was stabbed twice in the back, Davy."

Davy gazed at her in horror.

"Ben? Stabbed? But why? He had nothing worth stealing - and his wife is with child - Mistress Fosse - are you sure it was Ben?"

The serving girl stepped forward out of the shadowy corners of the room. Davy realized the weeping he had heard had been coming from her.. her eyes were reddened and her hands were twisted round each other ..

"It was Ben, sir," she faltered. "Master Cope identified his body."

Davy's stomach lurched, but he knew he must make the effort.

"Where is he now?" he asked, simply.

Mistress Fosse looked at his white face.

"What is he to you?" she asked.

"I grew up with Ben - we played and fought together as boys," Davy said. "I am come from Lydia specially - and I must see him."

"His body lies in the Chapel of Ease, All Hallows-next-the Abbey. The monks have washed him."

As Davy left Mistress Fosses's house, a tumult of emotions swept over him. The child had earned the coin, but Davy had no memory of giving it...he must have done so, for the coin was no longer in his hand. He led his horse towards the Abbey in a daze. How could this have happened to his friend.?

The afternoon sun lit the abbey door with a cold, wintry light. Davy tethered the horse near the old almshouse and walked slowly towards the great door of the Abbey. He knew he *had* to look at Ben - he had to see for himself what had been done - had he the courage? But had he the courage to face Lydia if he did not?

The Abbey was silent. He looked above his head, awed by the towering stonework and intricate carvings. Building was in progress at the East end of the Abbey, and Davy could hear the shouts of the masons and their workmen, and the hammerings and clatter of their work. He closed the heavy door behind him, and slipped through the narrowed opening which led into the Chapel of Ease where the townspeople worshipped. The Abbot had narrowed the opening significantly, and there would certainly not now be room for a processional to pass through into the Abbey. He glimpsed a kneeling figure at the foot of the makeshift bier, and slowly advanced towards the place where Ben had been laid. The monks or their lay workers had washed Ben and arranged his clothes decently. He was on a stone slab near the altar, and his hands had been arranged across his breast to hide the dark stain of blood which had spoiled his green tunic. His eyes had been closed and his dark hair was smooth and unmatted. His friend looked strange in death, as if he was carved in wax. The monk continued his vigil of prayer without turning; there was no-one else there.

Mistress Fosse had been right; this was indeed Benjamin Glover, lately apprenticed to Richard Cope.

Davy stumbled from the church, breathing unevenly. He was oblivious to the presence of the monk who had risen to his feet swiftly and followed Davy outside, and was now watching him darkly from just inside the shadowy door.

Davy leaned his head against the horse's flank, a half sob escaping him. He managed a confused prayer for the soul of his friend and then closed his eyes the better to see Ben's face clearly, eyes alight with mischief and fun, or watchful in the gathering dusk as they'd snared rabbits as young boys.

The brother watched him keenly, half hidden by the stone-work. When Davy finally felt more composed, mounted and rode off, the man moved swiftly to the back of the old almshouse and returned, mounted.

Davy was unaware that he was followed all the way to Lydia's house.

It was nearly dark when Davy returned to Milborne Port. He did not stop at Barton Holding, Instead he rode through the village to Ben's small cottage. He must see Lydia first.

Matthias Barton was relieved to see Davy on his return. Tracks to Sherborne were well marked; it was a central enough place in this part of the world, but after dark it became no better than any place in the Year of Our Lord 1436, and depending on the weather, tracks and pathways were not always easy to pass through.

Davy stabled the horse and came through the small courtyard to his own entrance. Elizabeth greeted him with a thankful cry, and then looked at his stricken face.

"It's not good news, is it.." she said quietly

"Hush, woman," he murmured and went straight to the solar, where he knew he would find Matthias.

Matthias had eased his long body down into a wooden chair near his hearth. His wine goblet was full and his relief at Davy's return was apparent.

"Ben is dead – stabbed through the back in two places." The bleak statement eased Davy's anger.

Matthias looked up at his man in disbelief. He was quick to notice Davy's eyes, black now with shock, his lips drawn together in a thin line to control his emotion. There was suppressed anger as well as grief shadowing his face.

"Ben is dead?" Matthias repeated the phrase stupidly, hardly believing what he had heard.

"He was found in the Lady Chapel..stabbed twice. He was fully dressed..exactly as I saw him leave here... the workmen found him when they started work... Mistress Fosse didn't know he had returned to the town. She thought he was still at home here until they called her..." Davy ran out of words in his distress.

"But what was Ben doing in the Abbey? He didn't work there, did he? He would have had no cause to be there... Someone in Sherborne must know more about this...he must have gone there deliberately.."

"I don't know, master, - he wasn't an Abbey man." Suddenly the fight was gone from Davy – it was as if a bladder of air had deflated and left an empty skin. He fought to control the tears which stung his eyes.

"Ben couldn't have had enemies, surely, he was always so amiable and friendly – I can't believe anyone could have done this to him."

Tears pricked the back of Matthias' eyes in sympathy for Davy as he poured a measure of wine and handed it to him.

"Did anyone send for the Coroner?" Matthias asked.

Davy shook his head. He had no idea. He had found Ben....he had seen the body...he had visited Lydia.... beside that, he had no idea what to do to be of any help.

"He must have become involved in something... something which had gone wrong. Someone needed to silence him... or just punish him but went too far." Matthias' quick brain had imagined scenarios which Davy could not even begin to forsee...Davy and Ben had lived a simple existence....village boys together. Davy was the older of the two and had looked out for Ben as they grew through boyhood to manhood...they had known each other all their lives. Now had arrived an unhappy parting of ways.

"Some-one had a plan for him, Davy" , Matthias said, quietly, "What I want to know is who? Why should a young man with apparently no enemies be found in a place so strange to him? Did he have information to deliver to some unknown person? That was odd in itself. How could anyone have latched on to a simple apprentice with a plan which was so deadly that it involved killing?"

"I wish I knew," Davy sighed. He was tired, and wanted nothing more now than to go to his own quarters and grieve for his friend.

"Get some rest, Davy," Matthias said, quietly. "Tomorrow we will ride down into Sherborne and have words with the Abbot's bailiff. He may be able to throw more light on this – if whatever Ben was involved in became a killing matter, we may need to watch out for Lydia."

On the night following the murder of Ben Glover, the Abbey Garden was silent. Brother Francis slept easily in his narrow bed; Abbot Bradford had prayed himself to sleep on his knees; there was no-one to see the silent watcher in the garden, who now knew where Ben had lived.

Chapter 3

Davy saddled their horses the next morning and both men armed themselves for the road. A thick fog was ideal for wolfheads, robbers and outlaws to way lay innocent travellers. Some of the unrest in the country as a whole was beginning to filter out into the country, and Matthias had no wish to be caught unawares if lawless men should take advantage of two riders.

The cold, grey wisps swirled round them as they left Milborne Port, first following the high track which joined Sherborne to Shaftesbury. Trees and bushes made weird shapes in the fog. It was a day with no colour – leaves and blades of grass were hung with beads of moisture.

The way was very open here. The dangers of the forest lay more to their South, where outlaws and discharged or deserting soldiers were to be found. Matthias felt the dampness seep into his very garb as they rode, with minute droplets of fog clinging to his eyelashes, making his nose run unpleasantly. The two men rode in silence, uneasy and troubled. There was little movement on the way, - one or two travellers making their way to the market with goods, but the fog and murky weather had discouraged movement.

In less than an hour they were riding into Cheap Street, the fog thinning a little round the shops and houses, revealing cobbles wet with fog and slippery with the refuse of humanity. The day was well begun

– Cheap Street was busy, despite the weather. The shop fronts were open for business, and the usual swirl of dogs, children and beggars thronged the narrow streets and the many side alleys. Here their senses were assailed by street cries, boys eager to hold their horses, beggars whining their needs and smells of baking, mingled with less pleasant odours as maid servants disposed of night soil. Matthias wrinkled his nose – Milborne Port smelled sweeter. A solitary monk, stepping carefully over refuse in open sandals, reached the corner of Hound Street as they rode by.

He turned to stare after them briefly, before disappearing in the direction of the Abbey.

They led their horses now, anxious to avoid the crowds going about their daily business., and aware of the confined streets lined by tall town houses. Matthias glimpsed several finely garbed young men, loitering round shoe makers, trying on the ridiculously long pointed slippers which had become the fashion...points of the shoes so long that they had to be tied to wrists for safety. He couldn't imagine what pleasure they gained for such impractical footwear....callow youths who were no doubt part of some noble household in the vicinity. They were loud and rude in their jostling, and Matthias was pleased to move on.

His first call was to Thomas Copeland. At present the schoolroom was in his own house in Cheap Street. He was busy with his scholarly duties, but Matthias was invited to wait in his small ante-hall. After the noise and smells of the street, he was glad to be in the relative peace of Thomas' house. He could hear the lazy hum of the town, muted by his now being inside; Davy waited outside and watched the horses, absently allowing his eyes to slide over the apprentices at the shop opposite, shaping leather into soft shoes with long, curling points in leather dyed in contrasting colours.. He guessed they must be nearing the end of their apprenticeship, for such work needed skill and craftsmanship. The young men they had seen previously had not yet reached that shop, so he was able to observe the colours and contrasts of the fabrics.

Thomas eventually freed himself for a few moments and joined Davy,

"So soon, Matthew?" enquired Thomas.

"I come on another errand entirely," Matthias told him.

"You've heard about the death in the Abbey?"

Thomas nodded gravely. He was well known to the monks and their establishment. They had in fact called on Thomas after the discovery to ask whether any of his scholars were missing.

"The body was that of Ben Glover," continued Matthias, "a friend and neighbour of my man, Davy."

Thomas raised his eyebrows in surprise.

"Whatever was he doing in the Abbey, then?" he asked.

"That is what I have come to try and find out," Matthias told him. "Ben was a young married man – his wife gave birth to their first child last night, and it seems to make no kind of sense to me at all."

Thomas looked Matthias squarely in the eye. "I don't believe the Abbot has called the coroner,"

Matthias frowned. "Why? Surely he should have done so as a matter of law." This was a serious breach ….how could the Abbot account for this failing? The coroner should have been informed immediately.

Thomas hesitated. He tried hard to be loyal to his employers, but the laxity of monastic life made it difficult for him to support their ways

He regarded Matthias silently. Matthias was animated, - even angry – and Thomas was aware that the zeal of the Abbot and the monks was not as it should be. They had grown lazy, too wealthy and complacent. It was inconvenient to have found a body in the Lady Chapel – no more than that, for it would have to be cleansed and re-consecrated. Thomas suspected they would make some superficial enquiries and then dismiss it as part of the animosity which had developed and was increasing between the townspeople and the abbey. He knew that the monks had washed and laid out Ben. He knew that even now they were waiting for Master Cope to claim the body of his apprentice and rid them of it. Were they alarmed that there appeared to have been a death in the Abbey? He thought not – it was merely dismissed as the result of a town brawl. He doubted whether they had given any thought as to whether Ben had any relatives who might mourn his death.

"The Abbot's bailiff might be involved," he volunteered. "Then perhaps you should visit Master Cope, who should at least be able to tell you of the arrangements for the removal of Ben's body, and if you find yourself in difficulty come back to me and I will try and help you. I am part town and part Abbey, so I can direct you to whoever you need to speak to."

Matthias left Davy with the horses and made his way up Cheap Street towards the top, where Master Cope had his house and his shop.

Some of the houses in Cheap Street were fine hall houses, mostly standing alone on a small plot of land,

and owned by the more prosperous merchants of the town. Some of them were next to alleys running through to the row of dwellings behind them, narrow runnels giving way to houses of lesser importance and wealth, hidden from view by the fine houses on the main street. Much of the town was built of fine Purbeck stone, but there were many less well built houses that were still cob and thatch, hidden from view in the narrower streets surrounding Cheap Street, the main thoroughfare.

Richard Cope was a master glove maker whose house stood nearly at the top of the steep rise of Cheap Street, almost opposite the Julienne Hospice. He employed four apprentices who were all at different stages of their seven year run; to begin with Ben had lived with him, as did the other boys, but when he and Lydia had married, he had arranged to lodge with Mistress Fosse from Monday to Saturday...Master Cope had been satisfied with Ben's work and as he had only a short time left to serve, the new arrangement had suited them both very well.

The small town was bustling with better trade as Matthias walked up the hill towards the top of the street. This end of Cheap Street contained the silver smiths, gold smiths and purveyors of fine cloths, leaving the lesser traders further down the hill. He kept one hand on his purse, fastened to his belt, for there were thieves and pickpockets even here, far away from busy cities. Street cries still assailed his ears, and the fragrant smell of baking made his mouth water as he passed the open front of the baker's shop half way up. The cellar of the Julienne Inn was open to the street, receiving casks of wine from an open cart....the carter impatient to be off to his next customer. Boys were working hard, rolling casks into the underground cellar by the trap door, which opened in the street. There were cloth merchants, fletchers, potters and glove makers in this part of the town, and Matthias strode past them, anxious to reach Master Cope's glove making shop. Glove making was a feature of Sherborne, and there were at least three other makers in the vicinity. Master Cope's establishment was nearly at the top, and Matthias was out of breath by the time he arrived there for Cheap Street was a steep climb.

Matthias found Master Cope in his shop. He was a vigorous man of heavy build, his florid complexion revealing his liking for fine wines, and his fine dark blue houpelandde speaking loudly of his prosperity.

"Good Morning, young man," the glover began, expansively, eying Matthias up as a prospective customer. He was about to wave one of his apprentices forward to continue to talk with Matthias, but Matthias forstalled him.

"I need to talk with you on a private matter," he said.

The glover's eyebrows shot up.

"What can a young man like yourself possibly want to talk with me about? I have no secrets."

Matthias was instantly alarmed at his mention of secrets...what on earth made the glover's mind leap to secrets so readily?

"I don't come here to speak of secrets," Matthias assured him. "I come here as a friend of Ben."

The merchant's face clouded and closed.

"I can tell you nothing," he said; Matthias noticed a nerve in his cheek twitch as the neck muscles taughtend.

"When did you first learn of his death?" Matthias asked.

"Early yesterday morning," The merchant told him. He looked away down the street as he spoke, and his eyes fixed on a distant spot as he replied.

"Why did you not send word to his family?" Matthias was puzzled by this lack of courtesy.

"I was waiting.." the glover tailed off, lamely.

"Waiting for what?" Matthias asked, puzzled. "Surely you knew he had a young wife who would be anxious, especially as her birth time was near."

Master Cope appeared to lose his concentration. His florid face reddened a little. He forced his eyes to look directly at Matthias.

"When in a guild, there are formalities to consider first," he declared, rather too loudly and pompously, Matthias thought.

"Besides, Ben was not working for me that day – he had taken leave. I did not consider myself responsible."

"But you have made arrangements now for his body to be conveyed back to Milborne Port?" Matthias persisted.

Richard Cope bowed his head in agreement.

"Do you know any more of his associates here in Sherborne?" Matthias asked.

The glover's eyes became wary.

"He is merely an apprentice, and one who has neared the end of his time, - why should I trouble myself with knowing his associates? He lodged with Mistress Fosse – he was a pleasant and hard working young man – beyond that I know nothing."

"Have you informed the Coroner of this death?" Matthias asked.

"That is not my responsibility." Richard Cope replied.

Matthias sighed, - he was achieving nothing. There seemed to be no point on which he could fasten to lead him forward, and yet he felt Master Cope knew more than he was uttering.

"May I speak with some of your other apprentices?" Matthias asked, casting around for any idea which might throw some light on Ben's last hours.

"There will be nothing they can tell you that I have not. Ben often delivered packages for me when goods were finished, - and he dealt with one or two minor customers - but this is really none of your business. It is enough that I have arranged the transport of his body to his home. What more would you expect of me? The other lads here are younger and had few direct dealings with Ben."

"Thankyou for your help, Master Cope," said Matthias, moving away from the shop, sadly. The glover was plainly uneasy, but Matthias failed to see why. As Matthias moved off, he returned to the shop and closed the door firmly. A monk opposite the shop nodded to himself and moved towards the glover's shop front, deliberately casual.

The fog had lifted a little as the serving girl of Mistress Fosse stepped into the street. She had a mission to accomplish which drove spears of ice into her heart, but do it she must.

Clasped in one hand was a key, copied to order by Ben. Ben would not be delivering it now to its destination, so Mary must do it.

Despite the fog, there were many people in the market in the nearby Shambles bartering for poultry. The stench of animal blood sickened her and she met several friends who also had kerchiefs pressed to their nose as they waited to be served, but Mary wasn't buying today. She had a different mission. She slipped hastily past them and turned right towards the Abbey, glad to be away from the slippery surface of the Shambles, and the cries of the poulterers. Today was a meat day....not every day was a meat eating day....strict rules still applied, so the Shambles was thronged with customers today.

The grey walls towered up in front of her, glistening with damp this morning, and as she passed the building work several of the workman whistled at her. Normally she would have looked up at them boldly for Mary was an attractive girl, but today her hair was coiled and hidden under a cap, and she picked up her blue fustian gown carefully as she picked her way amid the mud and animal excrement on the slippery cobbles.

Her heart pounded in her chest as she entered the Abbey by the Great West door. The silence seemed to whisper around her head, and she paused for a moment to gaze in wonder at the soaring roof and the mighty pillars holding such a roof. Within these walls one could feel small and insignificant... how little and unimportant one's daily life seemed. She crept softly towards the Lady Chapel. She felt a compulsion to see where Ben had been found...Ben, who had been kind to her so many times... he had been like an older brother to her. She had listened as he had told her of the coming baby...how he could use a little extra to buy soft woollen coverings for Lydia and the little one. A monk was praying near the spot where Ben must have fallen....her footsteps made little sound and she paused to try to remember a prayer for Ben's soul but panic overcame her. Her mouth felt dry as she went quietly down the far aisle and slipped out of a side door leading into the Abbey garden.

The fog rose and fell around her like an ethereal sea, mingling with her uneven breath as it hung in little clouds in front of her. She had never been in here before, and that made her more afraid, for she wasn't familiar with this area, nor even whether she was allowed to walk in this part of the Abbey. The trees were partly obscured from her view, and grasses and beads of moisture became one, soaking into the hem of her garments, sucked up into the fabric like a wick. She glanced round anxiously, imagining invisible eyes on her, but seeing no-one. She shivered, sensing danger.

The sounds of the masons working on the building were muted here and the isolation of the garden in this March mist was intense. A shiver of dread passed through Mary. Where had she been told to tell Ben to leave the key? She paused, listening. The dripping trees, leafless in this cold Spring seemed to shudder in the eerie stillness of the garden. Her mother's garden was a friendly place, - this was not so. The third tree from the monk's gate, yes, that was right - .Mary peered through the fog to find the monk's gate. Her eyes could not penetrate the gloom sufficiently to locate it......ah... there....she ran over the wet grass too fleetingly to avoid the granite stones hidden there, and fell headlong, grazing her elbow and jarring her wrists as she put out her hands to save herself. She clambered up awkwardly and stumbled on towards the tree she had been seeking... there was a cavity in the trunk. Mary's shaking fingers sought the rough bark of the cavity and she leaned against the wet tree trunk to regain her balance after the fall. Mistress Fosse would not be pleased at the mud on her gown, and she would have to mend the tear in the hem, already soaked by heavy dew.

So engrossed was Mary that she had failed to heed the monk from the Lady Chapel who had emerged from the Abbey and was waiting silently for her to deliver the package...

To her horror she realised too late that the key was no longer in her hand. Panic seized her. A glance over her shoulder told her what she had most feared........she had been seen in this garden, and by a monk! She did not dare retrace her steps to search for the key in the place where she had fallen. She would be in trouble now... he would report her to the Abbot. The Abbot would complain to Mistress Fosse and she would lose her position. Her Mother would be so angry... Mary turned towards the distant gate with no coherent thought but to escape and lifting up her skirts, took flight like a frightened bird, stumbling over the damp tussocks of grass. The monk moved faster than Mary. His long strides reached her before she even realised the pursuit. His hands, which had been plunged deeply into the sleeves of his habit, moved like lightning to sink the needle sharp dagger into her back. Only one accurate thrust was needed as she fell heavily and choked on a scream as the hot blood gargled up into her throat. She clawed the wet ground as she fell...... but her assailant was gone, retracing her steps to the tree. He plunged his hand into the cavity to retrieve the prize, but his hand met with nothing but wet twigs and damp moss. He had not seen Mary fall; he had followed her at a discreet distance and in a moment he was on his knees, feeling the surrounding grass with his bare hands. He wiped his dagger hastily on the grass as he heard approaching voices, and backed away through the garden retreating into the shadows, mentally marking her path for a more urgent search when there would be no danger of companions.

Unbeknown to him, the voices failed to materialise, their owners being directed elsewhere, and Mary lay dying in the silent garden with the cold March wind for company.

Chapter 4

Abbot Bradford tapped his fingers on the desk impatiently.

"What am I supposed to do about these petty complaints?" he asked, angrily.

He had listened with increasing anger to the catalogue of complaints from the brothers concerning the townspeople, and he was not a man to sit idle when his authority was being so directly flouted. This unseemly wrangling had begun in Abbot Brunyng's time, but was escalating now out of all proportion.

Today the townspeople had rung the bells of Allhallows at 6 a.m. The bells were especially loud and the ringing had seemed endless. Several old monks in the infirmary had woken, not to mention those brothers who had sung offices at 2.a.m.

"The new building work is being systematically interfered with by careless tramping.."

Brother Francis was chosen to carry the complaints to the Abbot, and he enjoyed his mission as he went on,

"..and the smoke from many heedlessly tended cooking fires drifts over the Abbey garden – preposterous!"

His final thrust was the ringing of the bells.

"They mock us, My Lord Abbot – we rise for services at regular times, but their bells ring out, breaking across the necessary contemplations we are so called to do."

Abbot Bradford sent for his scribe. His resulting letter to the Bishop of Salisbury was direct and detailed. In it, he entreated my Lord Bishop Robert to summon the townspeople and have them understand that these deliberate goads and annoyances must end, and they must abide by the recommendations of his public enquiry last November.

Two trusted lay brothers were summoned to horse, and the letter dispatched forthwith. In his few months as Abbot, there was, to be sure, much anger and animosity in this small town.

"Really, the dumping of the body in the Lady Chapel after a common brawl was the last straw," Abbot Bradford complained to Prior Simon. His expression was one of deep distaste. The two men were on their way to inspect the building works which were now making good progress after their enforced over-Wintering. They lifted their eyes skyward to inspect the scaffolding, and to watch some of the labourers carrying materials.

"These stones will endure long after we are gone," commented the Abbot with a great degree of satisfaction.

The stones were solid, cold to the touch and had an enduring appearance which inspired all who looked upon them to believe that this Abbey would certainly be a testament to the glory of God for several hundred years to come.

"If the culprit is apprehended, he will of course appear in the next Hundred Court?" Prior Simon asked, - it was a question, not a statement.

"Yes, if he is apprehended," conceded the Abbot.

"Have we informed the Coroner?" faltered the prior.

Abbot Bradford frowned. "We are not obliged to do so," he declared,

"Matters of the church are dealt with by church authorities."

"This was hardly a church matter," protested the prior. "The young man was a townsman."

"Absolutely," the Abbot confirmed, forcefully, "but I think we shall hear no more of it. Master Cope has caused the removal of the victim to his own home in Milborne Port. You see – he was not even a Sherborne man. That will be the end of the matter."

How very wrong he was – it was to be only a beginning.

The small town of Sherborne in the County of Dorset, was, like many others, built around the Abbey, - which had originally been a cathedral. The Abbot was answerable to the Bishop of Salisbury, - currently one Robert Neville, nephew to the late King Henry 1V- and both the abbey and the bishopric had become very wealthy.

They owned properties which were now rented out to small merchants who had benefited from the changing face of England . There was a prosperous cloth trade which was beginning to attract merchants from the South and West of England, and the Great Deer Park belonging to the Bishop of Salisbury stretched from just outside the small town and included Bishop's Caundle, Stour Caundle and Purse Caundle. The Abbot held sway over Sherborne and was landlord to many. The small town nestling under the towering presence of the Abbey was unimportant compared to Glastonbury or Shaftesbury, with the great religious orders dominating those towns, yet the Abbey had the town firmly in its grip, able to charge rents and taxes on so many different aspects of life.

The Bishop had both arable pastures and forest land in his domain, and as was the new custom, much of his land, and indeed, that of the Abbot, was rented out, thus making the demesne smaller. The income from pastures, farms, fulling mills, shops and individual properties was quite considerable and the good Benedictine brothers lived far more comfortably than several decades ago. True, much of the revenue was destined for the new building and the Glory of God, but the Benedictine community did very well out of it, nevertheless, and there was of course the income from the vast flocks of sheep which now grazed on the bishop's land.

Then there was the presence of the Castle, overlooking the town from its verdant position - the official residence of the Bishop of Salisbury whenever he had occasion to visit Sherborne. Built several centuries ago by Roger Caen, the castle had seen a stream of kings, servants of kings, and prisoners. It was showing signs of disrepair now, but housed visitors of the Bishop as well as itinerant soldiers in transit from the West Country to serve the king, wherever they were needed.

"What a disappointment the appointment of Father Samuel has been," The Abbot muttered to the Prior as they rounded the green which fronted the Abbey.

"I really thought his opinions would be to our good – he is too hot for the townspeople. I fear we receive little respect from him," he continued.

"He seems to have little regard for his own position when giving voice to his many grievances," agreed the Prior.

"An uneducated man, at best," concluded the Abbot.

"His utterances in the Latin tongue are poor and in some cases, quite meaningless."

"One of his grievances is that he is not able to conduct the Baptisms," Prior Simon said, softly. He knew this was likely to achieve the most effect with his superior; he was not wrong.

The Abbot's face mottled to an unlovely hue of purple. Spittle flew from his lips as he spoke.

"Never! Baptism is the most sacred blessing – and incidentally, one which is our revenue as a right. Baptisms are far too valuable a commodity to be performed by such an unprincipled man as Father Samuel. They will remain our prerogative."

"Do you think they will dare to use the font which they brought into Allhallows?"

"They were ordered by the Bishop of Salisbury to remove it," the Abbot hissed. He was becoming more and more venomous as the memory of the positioning of a new font in the chapel-of-ease came back to him.

"They will move it – I will not have it remain."

The positioning of a font in Allhallows was preposterous. It had been the final dagger thrust which brought the Bishop scurrying to Sherborne to hold his enquiry last Autumn, - and it had divided the townspeople, too. Certainly, Father Samuel was turning out to be too much of a champion of the people rather than the dutiful servant of the Abbot.

As the Abbot and Brother Simon turned to re-enter the Abbey at its great West door, they noticed Father Samuel approaching, a small band of townspeople with him.

"Good morning, Father Abbot."

"Good morning," replied the Abbot, coldly, not reducing his pace one jot. Father Samuel stepped slightly in front of the Abbot and jolted him to a halt.

"There will be the Easter processionals with baptisms soon," he announced, loudly enough for the crowd to hear.

"I'm glad to hear it," was the icy reply.

"I trust you will widen the doorway now that the labourers have returned, in time for the Easter processional?"

The Abbot made no reply. He raised his eyes and looked across the Abbey green towards the distant castle.

"I'm sure you will find a way to manage with the new and discreet doorway, Father Samuel."

The crowd behind drew nearer, a growl in their corporate throat. Fear of unpopularity was not one of Abbot Bradford's failings. He met Father Samuel's eyes, and saw a blazing fire of resentment in them. He held them squarely for a full minute before turning back into the Abbey to survey the mess the builders had left in the nave, Prior Simon following.

As he retreated from the confrontation, Father Samuel unclenched his fists. The crowd around him muttered sullenly before dispersing to carry news of the meeting to fellow men and women in the crowded market-place. It had hardly been the lengthy confrontation they had hoped for.

William Wass returned to his market stand, pondering on the unfairness of life. Sherborne was a good place to live – it was busy in itself with many attractive buildings; it was small enough not to warrant unwelcome attention from affairs of state; it had open and reasonably safe communication to Glastonbury, Exeter, Shaftesbury Salisbury and the coastal towns that allowed men to trade their wool and cloth with the continent - but the Abbey and the Bishop of Salisbury had become such powerful land-owners that although things were changing for the better, the townspeople still seemed restrained and in some way oppressed.

He sighed. He was a cloth maker, with cloth of good quality, dyed locally, and he was proud of his wares. He frequently took them to market in other small towns round about and he was proud to say he came from Sherborne, but his personal opinion was that the Abbot took too much for himself and gave too little of his time to the people. William's brother was a brewer, and he was sore annoyed at the payment of croukpenny to the Abbot – a tax levied on the brewing of beer. Henry would get himself into trouble sooner or later, thought William, if he insisted on being at the forefront of clandestine meetings among the fraternity of local brewers. He sighed again heavily, and turned back to his customers.

Prior Simon and Abbot Bradford had inspected their building works. The fog of early day had lifted, and a thin, watery sun had pierced the gloom of the clouds. The ground was still wet as they pursued their way back to the monastery by way of the orchard garden. Shafts of welcome sunlight arrowed their way through the bare branches of the trees, and beads of moisture clung to the hem of their robes. The low grey stone of the monastery was visible dimly through the remaining whisps of mist.

"The Lady Chapel must be cleansed and re-sanctified," the Abbot mused as they walked. Prior Simon nodded in agreement. "And the bailiff?" he asked, "Does he wish to investigate further?"

The Abbot sniffed dismissively.

"A town brawl – and not our concern, for it transpires that the young man lived in Milborne Port – not even in our own shire."

Prior Simon raised an eyebrow. He was of the private opinion that the Abbot was taking this episode very lightly. He did not choose to disagree with his superior however, the abbot being a proud man and of haughty demeanour. He tried again:

"But he was stabbed here, in Sherborne."

"Do we know that, brother? Have we proof? Do we want proof? Has anyone come asking for proof?"

Abbot Bradford cast a stern eye over his Prior. His gimlet eyes were bright with a passionate zeal which the Prior recognized as meaning that the subject was closed and not to be re-opened.

"Well," the other rejoined, doubt creeping into his voice as to the wisdom of making ripples where none seemed to exist.

They crossed towards the gate leading to the monastery; the fallen body of a girl became immediately visible.

"How did this townsperson enter here?" The Abbot exclaimed, hastening towards the still form. His sudden flaring anger reduced his reason. After all, who would be lying on damp grass from choice at this time of the year, - and on such a swirling, misty, inhospitable day?

But Prior Simon was ahead of him. He bent slowly to the lifeless body on the grass and gently made the sign of the cross, murmuring the words of absolution as he did so. Abbot Bradford's face blanched and his acid tongue was stilled.

"My Lord Abbot," said Prior Simon, as he carefully turned the girl to him to reveal the blood-soaked garments, "This girl is not here by chance, nor of her own choosing."

In his compassion, he closed the girls' eyes.

The wound was revealed as he moved her – blood had congealed and clotted around the middle of her back and the ground beneath had stained an ugly red, turning now to brown, - but above the entry hole, the black, sticky substance was visible. He turned away, covering his mouth with one hand as his gorge rose. He tasted bile in his mouth, and coughed awkwardly and discreetly to try and hide his revulsion.

"This is Bailiff's business," the Abbot declared.

"This is Coroner's business," the bailiff decided, kneeling on the grass beside the corpse. Rigor mortis was setting in, and the cold and damp had effected an unlovely puffiness to the girl's ice-cold skin. Sherborne was becoming a quarrelsome place, he thought privately. There was dissension among the townspeople, some of whom felt they should support the abbot in his decisions regarding the doorway, and affairs seemed to be getting overheated. But surely not enough to provoke murder?

For murder was what this second death most certainly was - and what of the first he thought, as he despatched messengers to summon the coroner. A tithing man from Abbot's Fee was sent to guard the corpse until Sir Tobias Delaware arrived – and guard it he did, - for two unhappy hours. Steven Lacy, the tithing man in question, was not happy to be asked to leave his shop on tithing business, but he had no choice. He left his wife and apprentice to manage the apothecary business in his absence.

The coroner arrived with his squire and a scribe, and trailing behind them, wringing her hands together and supported by Father Samuel, was Mistress Fosse.

The coroner was a commanding man who had served in the King's army against the French, and had seen sudden and ugly death in a far worse way, many times. This was nothing new to him, yet his manner was still courteous and gentle – unlike the Abbot, who was summoned from his house to greet Sir Tobias.

Sir Tobias took his duties as Coroner of Dorset very seriously. He was a well fleshed man of some fifty Summers, his dark hair showing streaks of silver here and there. He had keen eyes under bushy eyebrows, a straight nose and wore his trimmed beard with pride. His family life had taught him to care courteously for all cases in which he was involved; he took in the proud disdain of the Abbot, and the slight embarrassment of the prior, who felt his superior's attitude was unhelpful. The Coroner had heard of the Abbot's manner before.

"My good woman – stand a little way off and control this unseemly noise," he commanded. "Let the priest stand with her to comfort her."

He knelt on the damp ground and carefully removed the outer garment. A ragged tear where the blade had penetrated was apparent, and the power with which the blow had been struck had forced some strands of the fabric into the wound itself. He shook his head. The girl would have not expected this blow, - there was no evidence of resistance, and the wound was deep, implying force and strength.

Sir Tobias fingered the ground carefully around the corpse for any signs of the instrument of death, but there was nothing to be seen. He exchanged a quiet word with his squire, who was standing nearby, and both squire and scribe moved to search the surrounding area for signs of a discarded weapon. Very gently he lifted the skirt of her gown, but he need look no further – it was obvious that no rape or violation had taken place. The Abbot shuddered as he realised what had been in the Coroner's thoughts. He was silent. Chagrin was etched on his face as he remembered his harsh words to Prior Simon when they first discovered the girl, for although he was both proud and haughty, he was not malicious or unfeeling.

"Write your report, Sir Tobias, and have it conveyed to the sheriff. We must make ourselves available to you for investigation if that is what you would do"

"You saw no one on the scene as you approached?" The Coroner asked.

"The garden was deserted," The Abbot assured him.

"Take the cadaver to the chapel – wash and cleanse her, and keep guard over her until she may be returned to her family. I take it she has a family?"

"My lord, I must send word to the girl's family.." Mistress Fosse faltered, stepping forward and bobbing her head to Sir Tobias.

"And they live where?" he asked her, quietly.

"They have a small-holding in the village of Oborne, sir." She replied.

Father Samuel stepped forward, extending an arm to Mistress Fosse. He supported her by the elbow, compassionate and attentive, eyes lowered. He did not wish to appear confrontational towards Abbot Bradford under these unhappy circumstances. He forced his eyes to look towards the girl's lifeless form.... and found he was not as revolted as he should have been. He took in the scene – Mary was lying straightened now, as the coroner had left her, and her face was turned away from him.

"If you're ready, Mistress Fosse," he said, quietly, pressurizing her elbow slightly to indicate that they should be ready to move away.

Mistress Fosse allowed him to turn her away from the scene. They retraced their steps towards the side door of the Abbey, but his sandaled foot caught the same stone which had caused Mary to tumble. He felt ridiculous as he lay in the wet grass, nursing a grazed knee, but as he rose, he caught sight of a key, and without thinking or knowing what made him do so, he closed his fingers round it.. and slipped it into his scrip.

Three lay brothers from the monastery arrived to remove the serving girl, followed by two monks who would wash the cadaver and arrange it for burial.

"William," Sir Tobias addressed his squire, now beside him after a fruitless search for the weapon, "Ride to Oborne and seek the family. I would not want the maid's body to arrive before they are aware of her death. Watch and listen carefully to anything which jars....there must surely be a reason behind this killing."

To the Abbot he said "I understand this is the second such death in Sherborne within three days. I would like to have seen the first corpse. Why was I not informed of the killing?"

His tone indicated only too well what Prior Simon had feared – it should not have been ignored.

"It was the result of an unseemly town brawl, my lord." Abbot Bradford tried to sound re-assuring, but he knew he had no proof that this was so.

Sir Tobias frowned, and drew his dark red cloak more tightly around him to shield him from the chilly wind which cut across the Abbey garden suddenly. He was heartily glad of his fur lined hat and thick leather gloves.

Mistress Fosse had followed the sad little procession as they carried Mary back through the abbey, up the tumbled and messy nave with the builder's dross tossed hither and thither, and so through the narrowed entrance to Allhallow's Chapel of Ease

"How can you be sure that this was nothing more than a brawl?" Sir Tobias asked the Abbot, sternly. "Do you have so many deaths in Sherborne thus?"

"It was my considered opinion that this was an accident, - the first death," began the Abbot.

Sir Tobias scorched him with his eyes.

"And now you have a second death, following so closely on the first, - do you regard that as a town brawl, too?" His sarcasm was biting. "We have few deaths by violence in these parts at present. When there is such a death, you are required to report it to the Coroner – myself. You will not put yourself above that office."

Sir Tobias walked with Abbot Bradford to the gate of the abbey garden. His anger and disgust at the dilatory conduct of the Abbot was apparent. The sounds from the masons and stone-workers were still audible – in fact, seemed monstrously out of place in this still garden. There seemed no place for the distant careless laughter and chinking chisels and whistling men going about their daily lives, when here, one young life had been extinguished violently with a single stroke.

The grass was trampled where Mary had fallen. It was further flattened where Sir Tobias had knelt, and where the Abbot and his small party had stood and watched and wondered, but when they left, the garden was silent and deserted once more.

The silent watcher was surprised therefore, when he deemed it safe to slide furtively into the garden and feel again in the tree for the prize he had paid so dearly for… he too, was robed. The wet grass had soaked the hem of his garment, and his legs were cramped from waiting his chance to retrieve the key without being observed.

His face was grim as he retreated from the garden. His keen mind reflected on the presence of the party – Mistress Fosse, The Prior, Abbot Bradford, Father Samuel, The Coroner, his squire and his scribe, the tithing man Stephen Lacy, the attendant monks who had lifted the body, - had they removed anything from the girl? Had he missed something?

After so much patient waiting, he would not be double-crossed or thwarted.

Someone would pay for this disappearance

Chapter 5

Matthias was mixing ink and sharpening quills when news reached him of the second death. He laid down his knife carefully, and sat staring thoughtfully into the garden. Early Spring flowers were bending gracefully under a light wind, their delicate petals moved by the breeze, and there was sunlight in which today there was a hint of warmth. From this window he could see the roll of the pasture as it dipped down in front of the Saxon church to the meandering stream in the valley. His father had chosen wisely when he requested this piece of land for building – a quiet place on the borderland of two country shires – Milborne Port, the seat of medieval trading, just in Somerset, and Sherborne in Dorset.

When Milborne Port had bustled with traders from all over England and the continent, Matthias' great uncle had been the port reeve, responsible for fair commerce on the great trading days, but Milborne Port was retreating now, for times were changing; it was a quieter backwater now, its days of glory past. Wool fairs and continental silks and spices went to larger places, and even that less frequently now, since the wars with France.

Matthias put away his knife and locked the ink and horn books in a cupboard. Thomas Copeland had sent the message – now Matthias must act upon it.

He called to Davy to have his horse saddled – his house boasted a courtyard, at the back, where there was adequate stabling for three horses. Matthias only kept two – his own fine mount, and a nag for Davy to use. The largest stable was empty – his father's destrier he had sold before he went abroad, after his father died. He had no use for it, and it would have been too expensive to keep, especially idle. The beast had fetched a good price from a nobleman in Devon.

He found Elizabeth in the kitchen, which was at the back of the house opening onto a little enclosed garden where herbs grew.

"I have to go into Sherborne on business," he told her, "I'll be back before nightfall."

Elizabeth watched him go with a brooding eye.

"That's something to do with Ben's death, I'll be bound," she said to Davy, when he came in for a tool with which to strengthen the paddock gate.

"What makes you say that?" he asked, startled.

"A messenger came from Master Copeland. After a little, Master Barton just said he was going to Sherborne. He planned to be working here all day at the new school – he's had word from Master Copeland that needed more explanation – you'll see."

Davy put a comforting hand on Elizabeth's shoulder.

"Trust him to find out what he can," he said.

Thomas' message had been brief but succinct. There had been another death at the Abbey to which the coroner had been called. Matthias might learn more if he could catch the coroner before he moved out of the area.

He covered the distance between Milborne Port and Sherborne in less than an hour, and Thomas was able to tell him that Sir Tobias was staying at the George hostelry, at the top of Cheap Street.

Matthias wondered, as he walked up the hill, whether indeed Sir Tobias would see him at all – was it not an impertinence to ask questions about a second death – the only connection being that they had both been found in the Abbey.

Sir Tobias was dictating to his scribe in a small antechamber off the main parlour of the hostelry. The lady of the house had lit a fire for him, and he had wine at his side as he pondered the best way to report this death. The room was plain and rather cheerless, despite the fire, which didn't seem to want to burn brightly. It spurted sullenly in the dull grate, and from time to time, small acrid puffs of wood-smoke belched into the room in a bad-tempered way. There were several non-descript ornaments placed on the walled shelves, but the whole ambience of the room, unlike the rest of the place, was dispiriting. It was for this reason that Sir Tobias decided he would see his visitor, who might brighten up the morning a little.

As he faced Matthias, he felt his decision to have been a wise move. He saw a tall, slender young man in his mid twenties. His sombre dress seemed to be out of keeping with the vitality in his grey-green eyes, but although sombre, the cut of his garments marked him out to be a man of some standing. He was well-cloaked against the cold, and from his belted waist hung a purse and a sheathed dagger. Under the cloak he wore a woolen doublet of dark green, a suggestion of a white linen shirt beneath that, and warm dark hose were tucked well into riding boots with a small heel. The outstanding feature was his thick auburn hair .

No-one, having seen Matthias Barton could forget that head of hair! Despite his slim build, Sir Tobias detected an ease of movement that suggested fitness and vigour, yet in spite of all this, an air of solemnity and sorrow sat about the man now facing him, and nervousness also, for Matthias did not want to be thought interfering. However, he looked steadfastly into the older man's eyes, and for his part, saw a well-made man between forty and fifty Summers, wearing sensible yet fashionable garb; his dark red cote-hardie was belted at the hip, from which hung a heavy leather purse. Matthew glimpsed a fur lining on the cote-hardie - necessary for the wind was still cold. Sensible black hose and leather riding boots were planted in front of him, slightly apart, in a stance indicating self assurance and confidence – and yet the face held no hint of arrogance or impatience. It was a face lined with the weariness of war, - a face all too familiar to Matthias who had seen the same war-weary lines on his father's face on his return from the French battlefields. The nose was straight, the eyes warm and interested; Matthias thought he could well like this man.

"Well, Master Barton?" Sir Tobias barked, an affected impatience sharpening his voice deliberately, for he had no time for tale-bearers, time wasters and snoopers. "You asked to see me?"

He did not invite Matthias to sit down and Matthias, mindful of the need to be courteous to those of senior rank, stood respectfully in front of him.

"I would be grateful for some information on the death discovered in the Abbey yesterday," he began.

Sir Tobias raised his eyebrows.

"Indeed? And what makes you think you are entitled to this information?" he enquired, coldly.

His scribe, quill raised, watched the scene in fascination and anticipation. He had seen Sir Tobias in action for four years now, peppery when required, positively thunderous when roused in genuine anger.

"My serving man was a friend of the young man who was discovered in the Lady Chapel three days ago. His death was dismissed as a town brawl and was not adequately reported or dealt with."

Matthias glanced quickly at Sir Tobias as he uttered the mild criticism of the Abbot, but Sir Tobias was listening, bushy brows drawn together in sudden concentration.

"Ben Glover was not a man to brawl, nor had he connections in the Abbey. His wife gave birth to their first child two days ago, and Ben was desperate to be at the birth. Something is amiss here, my lord Coroner. May I ask whether this second death could throw any light on Ben's demise? I know not whether this second death was man woman or child; I am not a Sherborne man, and I was merely sent a hurried message…"

He stopped, striving to order his words. Sir Tobias put his elbows on the table in front of him, and tapped the tips of his fingers together. He frowned.

"You are not a Sherborne man you say, Master Barton. I was not informed officially of this first death – so where then, do you come from, Master Barton?"

"I have a house in Milborne Port, Sir Tobias."

"Milborne Port? Not even in Dorsetshire?"

"No, indeed, but I frequent Sherborne as a place I love – I was schooled by Thomas Copeland…"

Sir Tobias' face broke into a warm smile, showing teeth which were remarkably white and even for his age.

"Thomas Copeland? I know him well – I would like to think that my grandson would pass through his hands in the fullness of time - a thorough schoolmaster and a just and fair man – a good disciplinarian. So, - you were schooled by him?"

"Yes, before I went to the great colleges at Oxford – but Ben .."

"Ah, yes – Ben . Master Barton, it was a young woman whose body was found yesterday, so unless there is a connection it would certainly appear as if his death were the result of some town brawl – the girl was a serving girl in the home of a local widow lady."

Matthias' heart missed a beat.

" Mistress Fosse?" he enquired,

"Why, yes," Sir Tobias revealed. "Is there then, some connection?"

Matthias' face was both startled and puzzled.

"Mary was the serving girl in the house where Ben lodged during the week. He was apprenticed to Master Cope, the glover."

Sir Tobias thought rapidly as he gazed at Matthias' face, brow wrinkled in concern and distress at this new information. His attitude to Matthias altered.

"Sit down, Master Barton," he indicated a nearby chair. "Did you see the boy's body?"

"I did not sir, but Davy, my serving man did – he entered Allhallows to see Ben. He had been moved from the place of death and cleaned and laid out in a simple way, prior to being taken home to Milborne Port."

"Did he observe the wound?"

Matthias thought for a moment. He closed his eyes, the better to remember.

"Not very clearly. Davy was shocked – and there was a monk kneeling in attendance. It looked as if there was one wound only. His tunic was stained, and Davy's wife said when they dressed him for burial that there was a deep wound to his back."

"Is he buried yet?" asked Sir Tobias, sharply.

"Tomorrow, sir."

Sir Tobias stood up swiftly.

"Let us see his body at once.

They rode out together towards Milborne Port.

"There is little violent crime in these parts, thankfully," Sir Tobias mused, as they cantered on the trackway.

"Most of my work has been petty thefts, domestic quarrels and property disputes. These unexplained deaths make me uneasy."

"Ben was just an ordinary young man," Matthias told him, "Violent death isn't something I would have expected – not to anyone around here. It's a very quiet part of England."

"How well did you know him?" Sir Tobias asked.

"He is…I should say was.. a childhood friend of my serving man. They grew up together. Ben was a straightforward, fit and strong young man-recently married to his childhood sweetheart. I expect he had plans of his own to improve their standing – he had almost finished his apprenticeship to the Master glover, Richard Cope."

"Have you spoken with him?" Sir Tobias asked. They rounded a muddy patch of the track and Milborne Port hove into sight.

"I did so," Matthias admitted. "I hope that doesn't compromise your inquiry?" He was a little in awe of this man with his quick decisions and military air.

"No, - what did you ask him, Matthias?"

Matthias thought rapidly.

"Not very much really," he faltered. "I asked him why he hadn't contacted Lydia sooner, - that seemed to me to show a complete lack of feeling. He knew Ben had been killed, but he didn't send word to Lydia."

"And his reason?" Sir Tobias asked, looking keenly at Matthias,

"He couldn't really give a sound one. He hedged around a bit – said it wasn't his business to do so – something to do with the newly formed guilds – it didn't sound right to me at all."

"Did you ask him what kind of work Ben did for him – he must have been quite a useful and trusted fellow since he was the oldest apprentice there."

"Not in so many words," Matthias said, trying to remember Richard Cope's words.

"I think he indicated that Ben did some simple deliveries and some of the more intricate work for customers – I think Ben would have had access to customers, because at first, he thought I was a customer, and he was going to release me to one of his apprentices – it was only when I said that it was private business that he waved the young man away and we walked a little distance from the shop."

"Walked a little distance away?" Sir Tobias said, thoughtfully. "Perhaps that indicates that he may have expected you to speak of something else."

"His first words were that he didn't have any secrets," Matthias recollected.

"Maybe he didn't – maybe he saw more of Ben's agenda than he wanted to,"

"You mean he may suddenly have remembered an incident that might have had some bearing on the death?" Matthias asked.

"Exactly so," Sir Tobias decided.

"Didn't you think it strange that Ben should come home as arranged with Master Cope, and then go back into Sherborne? Did he own a horse?"

"Oh, no. He would have walked – he and Lydia were very simple people – no great possessions – just a tiny house and some furniture Ben had made – and yes, - it was strange, although I didn't know about it at the time. My man Davy told me after the body had been discovered."

"Your man Davy," mused Sir Tobias, "How close was he to Ben? Could he throw any light on Ben's sudden need to go back into Sherborne?"

"I don't think he knew, either, until Ben didn't return as expected." Matthias said. "Lydia came to Davy to ask him to walk out in case Ben was injured or had met thieves on the track. There was concern from Lydia, but not fear – not then."

They had arrived in Milborne Port, and Matthias turned the horses into his stable yard.

"Was there fear before the news of the death arrived?" Asked Sir Tobias, preparing to dismount.

"No, - I don't think so – great concern, but not fear. It wasn't something Lydia had expected at all."

"And this widow woman with whom Ben lodged.. what do you know of her?"

"Very little," Matthias replied, as Davy came out of the house to hold the horses

It was past two in the afternoon as they dismounted and waited while Davy tethered the horses, - Sir Tobias had requested that Davy should accompany them as they called on Lydia.

It was an unexpected call, and Lydia was over-awed by both Matthias and Sir Tobias. She curtseyed to Sir Tobias, and somewhat unwillingly, invited them both in. Her mother was with her, a small, shrunken woman, looking far older than her years, but strong in spirit and well in command of her grief for her daughter's husband, being herself no stranger to early death. The child was in a rush cradle in front of the fire in the one-roomed house, and the earth floor was well swept, although Matthias suspected that this was more the mother's doing than Lydia's, for Lydia herself seemed too worn out with weeping to have done any more than feed the little baby girl.

"We won't detain you long," Sir Tobias began, kindly, as Lydia's mother pulled a small wooden bench out for him to sit on.

"Abbot Bradford did not report this death to me, and I would like to look at your husband's body."

He waited for Lydia to make some response, but she remained silent, and Matthias could see she was striving to contain the tears welling in her eyes.

"Although you do not reside in Dorset, yet he was murdered in Dorset, and I should have been informed," Sir Tobias continued. "Is your husband's body in the church?"

Lydia nodded without speaking. Her mother spoke for her.

"His coffin lies in the church, sir. Please to go and look, although it won't help us now, will it?"

Sir Tobias Matthias and Davy crossed the green and entered the churchyard. A small dwelling on one side housed the priest, and Davy roused him to accompany them. He was serious and dignified, but Matthias could sense his aura of self importance as he escorted Sir Tobias into the church. The church at Milborne Port had stood already for three centuries. It had seen busier times and had been attendant on many griefs. The grey, square building with its squat Saxon tower exuded an air of solidarity and ordinariness.

The coffin lay near the altar, already nailed. The priest sketched a blessing and carefully undid the nails.

Ben had been tenderly dressed for burial. Lydia had been too distressed to do it herself, but the midwife had collected from Lydia the clothes she wanted Ben to be dressed in – his wedding tunic and best hose, points neatly fastened – and his hair carefully straightened.

He looked very waxen, Davy thought, holding his breath for fear of vomiting. He moved a little further away, and the priest moved with him, his face as waxen as Ben's.

Matthias and Sir Tobias eased Ben onto his left side, and pulled up his white woolen tunic. He had no undergarments on, so it was easy to see what Sir Tobias had come to see – his wounds. Sir Tobias was very experienced in examinations such as this – he peered closely, and Matthias held a candle at the angle directed by him.

"I think….I think possibly two different people…" he murmured, running his finger gently round the now congealed and crusted flesh at the wound point. It was slightly puffy, and the midwife had only skirted round the open flesh.

"There are two entries, very close together. They are at different angles and at different strengths. A dagger thrust leaves the character of its perpetrator, Matthias.

I cannot be sure, but I think Ben was attacked by two assailants, - and of course, from behind. He would have had no time to evade, and this seems to tell us that whoever he was expecting, he had no fear of them, nor any inkling that they would attack. They knew precisely where to attack for the surest kill, so they were not amateurs. If this had been a street brawl, I would have expected scratch marks on the body, and some evidence of marks on the front as he tried to ward off blows or thrusts, but there is nothing. Just two deep stabs very close together, - look – a bruise disfiguring his face – he fell heavily – and died almost at once, I should guess. I fear this is no town brawl. These were trained men who intended death .....but why?"

He motioned to Matthias to help him replace the coffin lid. It was a simple enough coffin, but fashioned from wood – no plain cloth shroud – and Matthias suspected that Davy had helped Lydia pay for the work – even simple coffins cost money. He must ask him and offer to help him with the cost.

Outside in the weak sunshine, they thanked the priest and rejoined Davy.

As they walked back to Lydia's simple house, Sir Tobias mused aloud.

"So, - Ben Glover lodged in the house of Mistress Fosse. Mistress Fosses' girl needed to go to the abbey garden following Ben's death – a place she did not usually frequent, according to Mistress Fosse. Why? Did she go to meet someone? To tell them of Ben's death, may be? She was killed in much the same way, although only one stab wound. Was there more than one person present? Or two? Did she know them? Or did they come upon her and catch her unaware?"

Davy shuddered. The very thought of walking alone in the isolated abbey garden in the fog...and some known or unknown person stalking up behind Mary and killing her – unshriven, alone and cold – abominated him. Suppose such a thing were to happen to Elizabeth?

"And why was Abbot Bradford so sure it was a town brawl?" Matthias asked.

"Now that's easy," Sir Tobias said, wryly, "The abbey and all its occupants have become lazy – and not just Sherborne – many abbeys, convents, monasteries – they've become too rich – too secular – they're more concerned with building wonderful buildings to the glory of God, filling their stomachs with the king's venison and taking rents and taxes to pay for it all."

Matthias was surprised by his outspokenness, but he knew it to be true – change had overtaken the monastic life, - and not unfortunately change for the better.

The March light was beginning to fade as they reached Barton Holding.

"I surmise that Ben did not realize that whatever it was he had become involved in, was quite serious. He had no fear of being attacked. He had no idea that whatever information he had might become a killing matter. He was, as you say, Matthias, quite a simple man. Darker secrets would not have occurred to him."

At the mention of darker secrets a shudder passed through Davy, and he was not surprised to hear Matthias' words to Sir Tobias.

"The way to Sherborne will soon be dark, Sir Tobias. Would you wish to stay until morning?"

Sir Tobias shook his head.

"If I leave now, 'tis but an hour's ride. I can be back at The George before full darkness, and I have my scribe lodged there. He will raise the alarm if I linger, - and I am also expecting my squire to return from Oborne. Besides, your wife will not be expecting a stranger to sup."

"I have no wife," Matthias told him, shortly. The Coroner raised an eyebrow.

"Through choice, Master Barton?"

"My father, mother and sisters all perished four years ago from the sweating sickness. I travelled to the continent to travel and forget- to plunge myself into an adventure that might help me to follow them. At last I made some sort of peace with God and returned home. I have been home less than a year."

Sir Tobias made no direct reply. He assimilated this information as if Matthias had merely commented on the weather. Inwardly he felt satisfied as to the cause of the underlying sadness in the younger man's demeanour.

As Davy brought Sir Tobias' horse towards him, Matthias turned. He spoke quietly, afraid of embarrassing Davy unduly, but needing to ask Davy when Elizabeth was not within hearing.

"How much did you give Lydia for the coffin, Davy?"

Davy raised troubled eyes to Matthias.

"I gave her nothing, Master Barton. Lydia found some gold coins in Ben's chest when she looked out his wedding garments. She didn't know he had them.. She paid for the coffin herself from the purse."

Sir Tobias was arrested, one foot in the stirrup. His hearing was very sharp, and Matthias hadn't spoken quietly enough.

"Say that again, Davy?"

"Lydia found gold coins in Ben's chest. She had no idea they were there."

Sir Tobias dismounted and faced Matthias and Davy.

"I want you to visit Lydia tomorrow and find out how much – and why did he hide it from her? Ben was being paid handsomely for services or information. I'll be at the George until I've visited the Abbot again."

As Matthias watched him ride away, he knew he had been right in believing there was reason to investigate further – and he also felt, with a glow of pleasure, that Sir Tobias trusted him to speak with Lydia. It was to mark the beginning of a long association.

Shortly after 8.o'clock the next morning, Davy left Barton Holding to attend Ben's funeral. He called at the house and accompanied Lydia and her mother on the short walk to church.

Matthias stood at the back of the church, wishing to pay his respects, but understanding that Lydia might feel uncomfortable at his presence.

After the burying, Lydia walked the short distance home, leaning heavily on Davy's arm. Elizabeth walked behind with Lydia's mother.

"Where did Ben get the gold?" Davy asked her, in a low voice.

"Davy – I don't know," Lydia replied desperately. "I only know I found it in a strange purse – even that wasn't Ben's. There's still some gold left."

Davy thought for a moment. Master Barton had told him what they needed to know, and warned him to question her carefully.

"Had he bought anything special lately? Any trinket for you over the last few months?

"No, he was very careful with money – we had nothing that was out of the ordinary."

"Lydia, - is it a large amount of money?"

Lydia was silent. She was afraid........afraid that Ben might have stolen it – afraid of what she might find out now that he was no longer here to defend himself. It was a large amount of money.

"Lydia, I must know. It may help us find who killed Ben and Mary."

Lydia stopped stock still and stared at Davy with dread in her eyes.

"Mary," she faltered, "Who is Mary?"

Davy clapped a hand to his head in despair. He wasn't quick witted like Master Barton – he'd forgotten that they had not told Lydia about the second death.

"The next day a serving girl was found stabbed in the Abbey garden. She was the serving girl of Mistress Fosse."

A little colour flooded back into Lydia's face.

"I thought you meant......." she was unable to put her thoughts into coherent words.

"You thought we'd lied to you and they were found together? No, Lydia – Ben wouldn't do that to you – he loved you dearly."

"So dearly that he was doing something dishonest?" Lydia cried, bitterly.

"Hush," Davy said, for Elizabeth and Lydia's mother were following closely and they had nearly reached the door of Lydia's home.

"Lend me the purse and the remainder of the money," Davy said. "Sir Tobias may be able to help if he sees the purse – Ben was not dishonest. I think he had stumbled on a way to earn money for you and the little one which somehow went very wrong for him."

Lydia fetched the purse, wrapped it in a clean cloth and handed it reluctantly to Davy.

"If it wasn't his to bring home, I don't want it back," she said, as Davy and Elizabeth left.

The gold glistened dully on Matthias' wooden table in the light of the tallow candles. The two men stared at it in bewilderment.

"There's still a lot of coin here," Matthias stated with a puzzled frown.

"That's a great deal of riches for Ben to have had – and there must have been more, for Lydia paid for the coffin with some of it."

The purse in which it was contained was of soft brown leather, quite unremarkable, except the quality of leather and workmanship was excellent. It certainly was not Ben's own – it was far too good a quality. Davy's face was serious in the flickering candle-light.

"Ben must have been involved in something dishonest, and rich men are mixed up in this somewhere."

He couldn't connect dishonest dealings with Ben somehow, - he'd always been so open and straightforward, - that is, until a short time ago. Davy remembered the occasion in the abbey when he'd found Ben very drunk. He'd told no-one about that. Where had Ben obtained the money to buy so much rich wine? And with whom had he been drinking?

"We'll go to the hostel in the morning and take the purse and its contents to Sir Tobias," Matthias decided, "and you need to think hard, Davy, of all the things you know – even unimportant things about Ben, that might show us how we can make some progress."

Davy slept badly that night, dreaming of Ben vomiting up his guts on the green outside the Abbey and when Davy finally managed to get him on his feet, Davy had promised to say nothing about the incident. Now Ben was dead, could he break his promise?

Chapter 6

Sir Tobias had completed his written report of the incident, and after a further visit to Abbot Bradford, announced his intentions of returning to his own home, first dispatching his squire to the Sheriff with the report. He wanted to see Matthias Barton again, and he was concerned by the information brought to him by his squire about Mary's family in Oborne.

According to William's story, the parents had been distraught, and were comforted by the three siblings of Mary, and the young priest from Oborne. However, when William had explained more fully the circumstances of Mary's death, the younger brother had slipped quietly away, and when William asked for details of Mary's movements, he was not present. At the time he had thought nothing of it, but as he was leaving Oborne, he glanced back at the house, and saw the boy- a lad of about twelve – slip out from a small copse of trees and run back into the house.

"Strange – we need to speak to him again," Sir Tobias decided.

Impatient to be home, Sir Tobias was ready to mount and leave when Matthias arrived, bearing the purse containing the gold.

"Ride with me, Matthias," Sir Tobias instructed, "I think we should look at this more closely."

Matthias was torn between returning to Milborne Port to continue his scholarly preparations, and falling in with Sir Tobias and observing how he would deal with the purse. Did it have a clue to yield up? He hoped so, after seeing Lydia's distress, and the youthful face of Mary, no more than fourteen years old, hopes crushed in a single stroke.

"I live at Purse Caundle," Sir Tobias told him, "Dine with us, and then we'll to business."

They rode in companiable silence for some distance, skirting the Bishop's great forest where deer offered plenty of sport – and good poaching, too.

Sir Tobias and his scribe were well seasoned horsemen, both armed for the journey, but no threats issued, and as they neared Purse Caundle, Matthias became anxious as to his part in this business. He was being drawn further in – and he had planned his life in a different direction. His school was due to open very soon, and he must complete the preparations.

Sir Tobias' family had held land at Purse Caundle for many years. Now much of it was let out to free men to farm as they wished in return for rent.

In his father's or grandfather's day he would have owned the men, who would not have been free to move, or even to marry off the manor, and who would have been obliged to give a certain number of working days each week to farm for him.

Change was rapidly taking place now. Since the fifth Henry had died the wars with France were not going so well, many things had changed. Soldiers were beginning to return to the countryside, starving, lordless, penniless, for wars were costly and the young king's coffers were empty – and in many cases the wandering men would be wounded as well. Fortunately in this part of rural Dorset, marauding groups of desperate soldiers were not a common sight, but talk was that they were now on the increase, particularly since King Henry V1 had only now become old enough to rule without protectors....... rumour had it that he was unready or unwilling to shed his protectors and had no stomach for war.. It was said that he found decision making difficult and preferred to read and pray. Sir Tobias hoped fervently that he would prove to be a strong king, or else this changing country would become lawless and dangerous with high born nobles struggling for power– and it could well spread even to this peaceful part of Dorset.

As they approached the house, a servant observed them coming, and ran to open the stout wooden gates. They rode into a cobbled courtyard, surrounded on all four sides by buildings in a pleasing golden, mellow stone. The sound of hooves on cobbles drew a stout ostler from the far side of the square to attend at once to the animals. Sir Tobias obviously commanded respect in his own home.

"The Lady Bridget is in the garden, Sir Tobias." He was told, respectfully.

"Come in, come in, Matthias," invited Sir Tobias.

Sir Tobias ushered Matthias through a side entrance into a cool parlour, and so on into a further long room, furnished with well hung tapestries, and a carpeted area near a great fireplace where a sweet smelling log fire was burning. This room definitely had the touch of a woman, and Matthias felt a sudden emptiness at his loss. His own home, - smaller of course, - was more austere. It lacked the warmth of colour.......the fire burned in the grate and a huge pottery bowl filled with dried lavender from last year's harvest was sufficiently near the grate to enable it to scent the room pleasantly. A dog barked in warning, and Sir Tobias called at once,

"Down, Muster!"

The dog, Muster, bounded in through the door which led to the garden. Matthias glimpsed it through the window – a glassed window, with little stained glass edging. The Lady Bridget had taste, - and not a little wealth.

She came in now, her dark green cloak edged with coney, worn over a heavier woollen gown. A girdle of light gold chains was round her waist, now thickening with age, and her greying hair showed slightly from under her simple veil. She carried Spring flowers in her hands, bent and muddied from the March winds.

"Well, husband!" she stated, a little breathless from striving to catch Muster, "I expected you last evening! And you, William –" here she stopped, -"Oh, my apologies, Sir – I thought you were William!"

Sir Tobias smiled.

"My dear, this is Matthias Barton, the son of the late Alexander Barton, of Milborne Port. He was schooled by Thomas Copeland – that admirable man to whom we look in the future for Luke's education. He has some information to impart to me that may be of help in this Sherborne killing and then I fear I must let him return to his own home."

Lady Bridget inclined her head, and Matthias bowed, courteously.

"Where is William?" enquired Lady Bridget.

"He has ridden to the sheriff at Dorchester with my report. We expect him tomorrow."

Lady Bridget left the two men to talk and work in this pleasing room. She was clearly well used to strangers appearing, Matthias thought, for she seemed satisfied with no more detailed explanation of his presence, and shortly afterwards, the steward brought wine and bread and cold meats, and a further log for the fire.

Matthias took the purse out of its cloth and laid it on the table in front of Sir Tobias.

"Lydia found this amongst some clothes of Ben's," he told the coroner.

"She's used some of it to pay for the coffin, - but she has no idea where it came from. She was horrified to think it could have some bearing on Ben's death."

He looked at it silently, turned it over and then shook the gold coins out onto the table. He turned the empty purse carefully in his square hands, lips pursed, and breathed out deeply.

"Do you know who owns this?" asked Matthias, as he watched the older man carefully.

Sir Tobias paused before answering.

"No, but When I was in France, several of my men came into possession of purses fashioned from leather as soft and supple as this. I believe the purse itself may come from France. Now this seems to say we are either dealing with a French spy – or we are seeking a soldier who has looted the purse as spoils of war. There is very little to spy out in this part of the country at present, - certainly from the king's point of view, anyway".

He turned the purse again, looking at every point of it.

"I think we are looking at something from France – not a looting spoil. The purse looks clean and is fairly new. Quite a common type of purse, but the style of the leather and stitching is not as we have in England. The contents – now, that's another matter. This is a great deal of money for Ben to have had. What was he doing – or giving – in exchange for it?"

Matthias shook his head. Davy had so far thrown no light on it.

"What connection might there be between Ben and the girl?" he asked. "Surely it is not co-incidence that Ben lodged in the house where she was a servant? And how could she be involved?"

"She knew something," Sir Tobias surmised, tapping a rhythm on the table, "something which would damage a plot or incriminate another person."

Matthias frowned, and tried to remember anything Davy might have said, but there was nothing.

"From what William said, there may be something in the family which connects them. The brother did not stay in the house, and was absent for all the time William was there. Go and visit, Matthias. Call at Oborne and look around. Talk to the young priest, - It's close to Milborne Port. Use some pretext – go and look for pupils, or wood for your fire, or a servant for your house. I think I shall return to the Abbey. There may be more to learn there."

Matthew fastened his riding cloak and rose to go. Sir Tobias called through a doorway to the ostler for Matthias' horse.

"When will you be in Sherborne again, Sir Tobias, if I need to contact you?"

"I must speak with the good Abbot again, and possibly his brothers – but I have other work to do as well. You are most welcome to ride over here again if you have anything of importance to add."

A child of some four years was playing on the grass outside the window where the Lady Bridget had been picking flowers, watched by a young woman of maybe twenty years. Her hooded cloak was pulled up to protect her head from the cold wind, but she turned to wave to Sir Tobias, and Matthias could see without doubt that this was his daughter, and the little boy was the grandson of whom he had spoken.

Sir Tobias answered the wave, and patted Matthias' mount..

"Alice and Luke are part of my other work," he revealed, with a warmth which Matthias envied. He himself should have been married by now, with maybe a son or daughter to delight his father and mother, as Alice and Luke were delighting Sir Tobias and Lady Bridget.

Somehow he must engross himself once again in his school plans, or his new found sense of direction would crumble around him.

Elizabeth had lit a fire, and Matthias was grateful for its glow. The logs Davy had split were spitting and crackling – the sap or resin was still damp and the crackling noise made it impossible for Matthias to relax. He stretched his legs before the fire, and tried to let his mind wander. He was drifting into an uneasy sleep when Davy's knock at the door startled him awake.

"What is it, Davy?"

"Master – the day did not go well here."

It was a bald statement which needed further embellishment.

"Come and sit down, Davy."

Davy sat on the edge of a wooden chair uncomfort-ably, far away from the fire. He had been with Matthias' family for all his working life, but he was aware of social differences, and Matthias' father had never invited closeness, although Davy'd been only a stable lad of twelve then. The age difference between himself and Matthias made no difference to the social gulf between them.

"What went amiss, Davy?" Matthias enquired.

"A stranger came through the village seeking Lydia's house. He marked it well, but he didn't call on her – just rode away. I was out at market with Elizabeth, and I heard him ask people where Ben Glover's house was. I didn't like the look of him, so I said nothing. It was Walter Meer who pointed out the house to him. Elizabeth was going to speak, but I silenced her – and when he just nodded and rode away without smiling or thanking Walter, I was glad I had remained silent, for it meant he would know us again."

"What did this stranger look like, Davy?"

"Sullen – not a mannered man, yet well dressed. His speech was more clipped than ours – ours is broad and easy. He had dark hair and a fashionable beard, - not a poor man, I fancy, because his tunic and hose were of good quality cloth, and his riding cloak and hat were trimmed with fur."

Some inner sense of danger he was not aware he had, prickled at Matthias' spine.

"Davy, do you think they could be looking for the gold? Perhaps he gave it to Ben in the first place, and is anxious lest it be found and leads to a trail of discovery."

"I think it may be likely, Master Barton."

"Where does Lydia sleep?"

"Near the fire in her downstairs room on a truckle, and I expect her daughter now sleeps beside her."

"Is her mother still with her?"

"Not at night, she returns to her own home before nightfall."

Matthias made a decision.

"Davy, I'm afraid for Lydia. Will you watch the house with me tonight?"

"Gladly, master," replied Davy.

It was wisdom which prompted Matthias and Davy to leave Barton Holding before darkness fell. They were both armed with daggers slung from their belts, and both dressed in dark hose and tunics with hooded cloaks. In the absence of Davy owning such a garment, Matthias had remembered his father's chest, and had loaned Davy his father's woollen cloak.

Because it was not yet fully dark, the two men were able to walk freely through the village without subterfuge. Lydia's house stood on the end of a row of similar small dwellings, mainly made from wattle and daub, with simple thatched roofs. The houses here were close together, and the street which ran down the middle was narrow, with a gutter running down the middle where refuse was thrown.

The clouds were dark in the sky as Matthias looked up at the outline of the bare trees which edged this end of the village. He had made no plans beyond watching the house to make sure that no harm came to Lydia. Now he suddenly felt small and rather childish. What did he think he was doing, creeping around at night?

Where could they conceal themselves and still be sure of seeing Lydia's house?

He was filled with a quick rush of depression, but Davy surprisingly turned left opposite the end cottage and Matthew found himself pressed into a doorway.

"This house is empty," Davy said quietly.

"It lies opposite Lydia's, so we should be able to see if anyone approaches."

Cold seeped into Matthias' very bones as they waited, crushed hard against the door, half sitting on a broken earth step. Few people ventured out after dark at this end of the village. Money didn't run to excess ale very often in this quarter, nor to warm woollen cloaks against the bitter night wind. Children cried distantly from inside nearby houses, and once they heard voices raised in fierce argument, but apart from that, the darkness and silence was complete. Silence was bleak, cold and sinister. Matthias became too chilled to sleep. His limbs were cramped from being so still, and his ears ached fiercely with the cold. He lost all sense of time – two hours.......maybe three – and he and Davy had not spoken in all that time. Matthias flexed his tortured muscles and prepared to stand, to give his body a chance to recover some feeling, but Davy's fingers gripped his arm and bade him be still.

They sensed, rather than saw, a shape materialize in the darkness...move slowly round to the side of the end house, holding the wall as he moved, the better to quieten his feet. He seemed to steady himself on the corner of the house.

Matthias could not see what he was doing – there was some fumbling, and for a moment it appeared to be nothing more than a cloaked and cowled figure who had broken all vows of abstinence. Then the figure moved out into the centre of the narrow trackway and slightly out of their vision.

Davy leaned forward to try and see what direction he had taken, when the stillness of the night was broken by a heavy twanging sound, and a fire arrow was shot into the air with deadly accuracy and pierced the thatch of Lydia's cottage. Davy shouted, and the figure came back into view, picked up his skirted gown and ran, Davy in hot pursuit, towards the open space of the village green.

Davy was gaining on him as they reached the open space of the green, but from the trees a second figure emerged, holding two horses. Davy scarcely had time to think – he saw the second figure drop the reins and draw a bow, and he flung himself to the ground. The arrow zipped over him at some speed and thudded into the ground just feet beyond where Davy lay. He heard the thunder of hooves on the ground and the irregular beat as the horses were turned. He had time to glance to see in which direction they were facing, only to realise in horror that they had turned towards him, and were intending to trample him.

He rolled himself into a ball, wound his arms round his head, terrified of the pain to come. He shut his eyes........ heard a shout...another shout behind him... the whistle of a missile flying through the air....whinny-ing of frightened horses...a shouted curse and then felt the thunder and vibration as the horses veered away from him without reaching him and back through the wood, then he heard Matthias shout "Fire! Fire!"

Davy scrambled to his feet, dizzy and trembling from his ordeal, but fearful for Lydia. Those great horses would surely have trampled him to death. Who were these people, - what did they want, and how had they come to be so involved in this tangle of evil intent against innocent people?

The fire arrow had ignited the thatch and it was spreading well. Greedy yellow flames were licking the thatch, biting into the night sky.

Men began to emerge from neighbouring houses, rubbing their eyes, pulling sacks round them to cover their night nakedness – and then suddenly awake to the danger – desperate to stop the fire spreading. Some had water in troughs at the back of their houses ready for morning, and they quickly brought it, slopping it in their hurry to save not Lydia's – that was burning well now, - but their own. Their primitive houses were tinder dry and flames would take hold so fast, so very fast.

Matthias put a shoulder to Lydia's latched and bolted door. It gave easily, and she was visible in the flickering light of the hungry flames – her night shift too thin to combat the cold outside, and her hair loose and tousled from sleep. She was clutching her little daughter protectively to her breast. Davy grasped her hand.

"Lydia, - it's me, - Davy, some-one has fired your roof – come!"

"Where shall I go? What shall I do?"

"Bring the babe – there's no time to lose!"

Her relief at hearing Davy's voice was palpable. She had feared marauding robbers who would know there was no man in the house.

Matthias picked up the empty cradle in his arms and followed Davy and Lydia out of the burning house. As he left, Matthias saw the worn thatch fluttering down in burning strands to fire the poor interior, which would in turn engulf the wooden structure of the house.

There was a crowd of villagers outside now. Some had spades and were beating at the burning straw; others had water. A little breeze carried the scarlet, glowing sparks into the air, spelling terrible danger for the rest of the row of houses. Matthias thought it looked like a scene from hell itself.

Lydia's house burned quickly. The house next to it was luckier. Because the alarm had been raised so promptly, the smouldering straws were being extinguished, and although the roof was damp, it was really only Lydia's house which was past redemption.

Davy drew Lydia to him.

"Come – let's get away from here."

He looked at Matthias, who nodded. Lydia's neighbours were totally absorbed in saving their own houses, and her mother had not yet appeared.

By the time they thought to care for Lydia she had gone with Davy to Master Barton's house, where Elizabeth gave up her own bed for her.

Matthias ached in every limb. Whatever they had expected that night, it had certainly not been this. Lydia was safe under his roof, with her child; Davy was bruised and shocked; they had been shot at by two men who had tried to kill Lydia and her child, and all parties were dirty beyond belief.

Matthias knew he had to return to Purse Caundle in the morning.

Chapter 7

Davy roused Matthias at daybreak. Matthias noted that Davy was moving stiffly, as if he ached, and that one side of his face was grazed where he had flung himself down on the ground.

He felt stale and tired. He unlocked his cupboard and took out ink and parchment, and listed events, but he stared at what he had written unseeingly. His eyes ached, his head was fuzzy, and his clothes smelled of smoke. The depression of the previous evening had returned. It all looked so dull, so lifeless – even pointless.

He had not felt like this since his return from Italy. He must shake this off – nothing made sense. There seemed no link – no pattern. How would you even go about finding a pattern? And how had he allowed himself to become involved in this? He would go this morning, after he had washed and changed into fresh clothes, and tell Sir Tobias of the new development, and make it clear to him that he, Matthias Barton, had business of his own to attend to. He really couldn't divert his attention any further away from his chosen course of action.

Having decided on this, he washed and changed and had Davy saddle his horse.

"I'm going to see Sir Tobias, Davy. Lydia is welcome here, but she may prefer to be with her mother. You and

Elizabeth are free to do as you wish with her. I cannot turn her away homeless."

"Thank you, ," Davy replied.

As he rode away, he reflected on the wisdom of his generosity. Although his house was a family house, he could not help but feel that he would regret Lydia's presence – a baby crying at all hours, and having to find Lydia some sort of work to do – and she would be taking up room that he might need for his scholars.

He first went to Sherborne, for he remembered that Sir Tobias intended visiting the Abbot again, and Sherborne was a more direct route than Purse Caundle

He hesitated as he entered Sherborne. He couldn't go again to Thomas Copeland who had his own work to do. Should he go to the Abbey?

He was leading his horse towards the abbey, past the progressing building works, when he chanced across Mistress Fosse. He did not know her well – he had only seen her once, at Mary's burying. She was talking earnestly to a lad of some twelve or thirteen years, and Matthias deliberately slowed his horse and made as if to pick something from the hooves.

"You are welcome to look at Mary's room," she was saying, "But I have cleared it in readiness for a new maid-servant, and I am sure nothing was left behind. She had very few belongings, and her clothes and trinkets have all been returned to your mother."

TO YOUR MOTHER! This was Mary's brother – must indeed be the youth who had absented himself to avoid being questioned – or recognized. The pair passed him without a second look, through the Shambles and towards Mistress Fosses' house.

Thoughtfully Matthias turned his horse and followed at a discreet distance. He tossed the reins to a young boy in the market place, first showing him the coin he would have on his return if he minded the beast – and set out on foot.

They went a fairly short distance into Hound Street. It was now drizzling lightly, and Matthias became aware of his hair gathering a layer of light moisture, and his collar becoming damp – an unpleasant feeling on an equally unpleasant morning, which did nothing to lighten his mood of despair.

Mary's brother was not long in the house. Mistress Fosse closed the door very firmly, and the youth stood outside irresolutely, looking downcast and disappointed.

Matthias decided to approach him and challenge him – he had nothing to lose, but before he could do so, two monks detached themselves from the corner of the street and paced purposefully towards the boy. He saw them and turned to run; they were too quick for him, and Matthias tried to keep pace with them as naturally as he could, without appearing to follow. The youth was being frog-marched along the cobbles, stumbling every so often.

The long strides and the apparent surprising strength of the two monks made following unobserved very hard, and Matthias reluctantly allowed them to gain space. From their assured physical strength he was pretty sure they must have been the two figures he had seen at Lydia's home last night – and they clearly wanted something from the boy.

Matthias tried to keep them in sight, but they were pounding hard towards Newland, half running, half dragging their unwilling companion. In the drizzle, now turning to a steadier rain, Matthias was delayed by some ale casks being rolled from the brewers and loaded onto a cart – and when he managed to pass, there was no sign of the three figures.

Matthias stood for several minutes, puzzled by their sudden disappearance. He hadn't been delayed for more than two or three minutes, but whichever way he turned, there was no trace of the little party.

With the rain now plastering his uncovered head, Matthias trudged wearily back down Hound Street, cut through an alley and came into Long Street, and so into the Market Place.

Traders looked wet and dejected; few maidservants and their mistresses would venture out now unless they had to – men pulled Hessian and rough cloths over themselves to try and protect themselves from the worst of the rain. The boy holding Matthias' horse was sheltering under the wooden arch of an ale house. Matthias gave him his promised coin, and the ragged arsed child ran off, bare feet splashing through the puddles in the uneven cobbles.

Matthias felt unbearably tired. The rain now streamed from his horse, was soaking into his garments and he had no plans now for any action. He rode dispiritedly towards the Abbey. The masons and their labourers were sheltering – some in the building works under scaffolding, and others making their way into the nave. Matthias rode past, and on a sudden whim, turned his horse into the monastery gates.

It was the duty of the monastery to give comfort to travellers, and he was tired, soaked through and could certainly describe himself as a traveller in need.

He was admitted to the guest hall by the chamberlain monk, whose responsibility it was to oversee the hospitality towards strangers, and when his horse had been stabled by a lay brother, he sat by the fire in the guest hall, his clothes steaming. An elderly monk brought him bread and pottage in a trencher, fragrant with herbs and smelling deliciously gamey. The monastery had many lay workers as well as twenty-four monks – in fact they had a whole multitude of servants these days, and their table was well furnished with game, fish from their own stew ponds, poultry from their own farms and lamb from their own flocks.

There was no other person in the guest hall at that time, and Matthias, on a high backed wooden settle, dozed after his disturbed night and enforced walking of the morning.

He became dimly aware that other travellers had joined him…Brother Francis bringing more food for the other guests…..the presence of other people….more logs being fed to the welcome fire. He knew he must move soon. It was not his intention to stay overnight, and he was too tired and it was too late now to ride out to Purse Caundle to see Sir Tobias. His depression had not lifted; he was involved in something too difficult for him to penetrate; he was not a fighting man, although he was fit and young; he was failing himself for not pursuing his decision to open the school within the month – he had wasted too much time on the affairs of other people - and yet he was a man who could not tolerate injustice, despite his overwhelming feeling that life had been less than just to him.

Lydia's tragedy was unjust; Mary's death was callous and ruthless – and Sir Tobias had warned against allowing law and order to fall into disrepute.

Men were becoming dissatisfied with their lot and were greedy for more power in their own lives. Tradesmen were finding ways to become rich and call themselves merchants – and men, and women, too, were wanting more from life than they had had in the past. Wasn't that why he was opening a schoolroom? Tradesmen knew that their sons could better their lives in the future, but they would need to be able to read, to calculate their earnings, and to write. The way forward had to be through education, but education cost money.

It was all a never ending circular trap, thought Matthias, wearily. He pulled himself back from half sleep with an effort. The fire hissed gently on the vast grate in the centre of the room. Murmured conversation from other travellers behind him washed over his consciousness... words which meant nothing to him at first.

"There was no sign of it near the girl."

"Her house was burned to the ground, - no chance of any discovery there."

"If it was in the house, it's certainly burned to pieces now. We saw to that alright."

"The young man needs careful watching – he was near her house that night

"Would you know him again?"

"Oh, yes. I know him. I don't know how he's come to be involved, but he needs watching."

"It was foolish to kill the girl so soon – quite unnecessary."

"Don't know how much she knew."

"Can't get anything out of the boy."

Suddenly alert, Matthias moved his head, trying to focus his eyes without turning round and drawing attention to himself. They said they could recognize the man. Was he the man, or were they talking about Davy? He had no way of knowing.

Two well dressed travellers of merchant class were conversing softly together quite close to Matthias. One had a small dark beard, and there was a third man with his back to Matthias.

"How much do you think the Glover knows?"

"Hard to say – watch the shop for a day or two."

He closed his eyes again, alert now, but the conversation had died away. After a suitable interval, Matthias stood up and stretched lazily. His clothes had dried, although he felt dirty and unkempt. Without apparently glancing in their direction, Matthias strode out towards the stables. His horse was there, and whilst the boy saddled him, Matthias was able to look over the other mounts now in the stable. There were several, but he thought he recognized one by the size, - he'd seen it rear up and thunder towards Davy before he'd hurled stones at it.

He dared not return to the hall to have a closer look at the three men for fear of being recognized – and it might be that he was the man they'd been talking about. He hoped it was Davy , for there was no way of disguising his own distinctive auburn hair.

If they were the men who had attacked Lydia's house, they might well have had a good view of himself as he'd hurled stones, and to be recognized would spoil his chances of helping Sir Tobias.

Matthias mounted his horse thoughtfully and trotted up Cheap Street to join the well worn track towards Shaftesbury which would pass through Milborne Port. What was it that these men wanted from the brother, or from Mary? How had Ben become involved? There was obviously a piece of information missing from their information. Mary, her brother and Ben were linked to something dangerous – dangerous enough for murder.

He felt he might be a little closer to a thread of truth, although right now he needed a change of clothes, a talk with Davy to clear his mind, and then tomorrow without further delay, a ride to Purse Caundle.

In the guest hall, one of the three men stood up after a suitable space of time. He looked round at the remaining guests, satisfied that there had been no-one with his quarry.

"He'll be on his way home now," he announced, "No need to track him this day, but if he has what we're looking for, his day of reckoning will come – and soon."

His grim tone belied his pleasant boyish face. His companions laughed, - a sound without warmth or humour.

"How can you be sure he didn't overhear us?" one asked.

"He was sleeping – a soft touch youth after a little ride to Purse Caundle"

"Be patient, you told us," the bearded man said, "But how long, in this cold, inhospitable place?"

"I've stayed my hand for two years," the younger man replied. "To be thought local and to build trust takes time."

The two older men faded away towards Cheap Street, merging into the darkness of the night, whilst the younger man mounted his horse and rode thoughtfully up the hill. following in the same direction as that which Matthias had taken.

It was dusk before Matthias reached Barton Holding, and he found Davy conversing with a stranger outside the house.

"Father Peter, from Oborne," Davy explained, by way of introduction. The priest nodded a greeting to Matthias.

"I was seeking the friend whose childhood companion was found murdered in the Abbey," he told Matthias, "and," he continued, looking kindly towards Davy, "I have found him with little trouble. As Mary's family are distressed, so must you be."

Matthias was puzzled by his concern and interest, but his next words showed a clear path to his purpose.

"Mary's mother asked me to bring this small package to you, in order to deliver it to Ben's wife. Mary had made a small gift for the coming baby, and her mother was most insistent that it should be delivered. Here-" and he held out a roughly wrapped package. Davy took it from him solemnly.

"Thankyou, Sir," he said, quietly. "I will give this to Lydia myself."

Father Peter sketched a blessing over the two men and mounted his horse.

"We may meet again before this business reaches closure," he said, as he rode off.

Matthias felt that at least some good had come of the day at its close.

Chapter 8

Matthias rode off to Purse Caundle early next morning. He had talked long with Davy on his return home, and the more he talked, the more Matthias became aware of a sense of shame in himself. What he had learned that day was most valuable, but he had wallowed in fatigue and self pity. The events of the previous night, too, were most disturbing, and he had delayed going over to Purse Caundle with this new information. That was valuable time lost due to his own inaction. He instructed Davy to ride to Oborne to try and find the boy, and he himself started at first light on the road to Sir Tobias' house.

After Matthias had left, Davy saddled the nag, and leaving the work of the school until later in the day, set out to ride to Oborne. He rode the nag carefully; the trackway had become wet and muddy, and further more, he needed to think over his approach to the visit.

It would seem likely that the two monks had marched the lad back to Oborne to insist on a further search for whatever they were searching for. That was yesterday. It was clear now that it was not the purse of gold coins.. Would the boy still be there? Once it was found, would they dispose of the boy, as they had apparently despatched his older sister?

There was another problem on his mind, too. Should he tell Master Barton about the drunken episode? Was it important? Could you break your word to a dead man?

He passed several carters on the track, for today was Wednesday and the brewers of Sherborne sent their casks out on a Wednesday, but he saw no-one of any importance, and as he rode towards Oborne, keeping the little stream on one side of him, he pondered nervously how to fulfil his task successfully – he was not a quick thinking man, given to using made-up stories. Perhaps his encounter with the young priest might be of value to him.

Matthias had concocted a story for him to use. Lydia had mislaid a belt which she had given to Ben , and he'd been sent to enquire whether it may have been mistakenly given to Mary's parents with her other belongings. Davy hoped it didn't all sound too thin.

Oborne was a small vill, hardly half a dozen cottages, some farmland and the church. Like Milborne Port, the church had stood for many years, short and fat, brooding over the small cluster of houses. A tributary of the River Yeo ran through the vill, providing clear, fresh water. The main occupation was, as in so many places in South West England now, the rearing and tending of sheep. Vast flocks were grazed on these chalklands, owned by great landowners – the Bishop of Salisbury, The Abbot of Glastonbury, The Abbess of Shaftesbury – sheep grazed wherever you cared to look. The good people of Oborne simply kept alive by growing vegetables and tending the flock

Davy easily identified Mary's family dwelling from the description with which William had provided Sir Tobias . He tethered the nag some distance away, and leaned on a gate by the clear stream to watch for a few minutes.

Oborne lay on a flat piece of land, pastures rising up behind it, with a wooded area behind the church on a steep little rise. The few houses were clustered together, mostly wood framed with wattle and daub, and all with a thin strip of land beside, for growing vegetables. In the furthest one Davy could see a small herd of pigs being driven up into the woodland to forage. A lad of some seven or eight years was driving them with a switch of hazel wood.

From behind, a voice made him jump.

"We met last evening, Sir. Can I direct you?"

Davy turned nervously; it was the young priest.

"I'm looking for Mary's house, Father, she who was recently killed in Sherborne."

The priest regarded him silently. He was a young man, appointed by the Abbot a year or so ago. He watched Davy with what seemed like mild amusement as Davy's colour rose at the lie. As Father Peter remained silent, Davy stumbled on with his story

"I'm a messenger for Ben's wife - he who was murdered in the Abbey before Mary – you came to see us but yesterday, so you know..... His wife had a missing belt when his belongings came back – she gave it to him as a gift – Lydia is hoping it is tumbled in with Mary's things."

It sounded lame and contrived. Davy was unused to such stories.

The young priest smiled.

"You should have mentioned it last evening. I could have saved you the journey. Mary's parent's house is the third along from the ford. I hope you find what you are seeking .

"Lydia came to me with her loss only this morning," Davy mumbled, by way of explanation.

He stumbled down the slight hill to the cottage which he had identified himself, without the priest's directions. He felt hot and confused as he left the young man. He was not good at telling untruths or elaborating stories. He was a good, honest, straightforward man with no guile; he had not enjoyed his implied dishonesty to a man of God.

A few scrawny fowls scratched in the semi-tended garden. The cottage bore an air of defeat. A girl of ten or eleven years was visible in the open doorway, carding last year's fleece.

"Is your mother here?" Davy asked her.

The girl stared up at him with brown, tear-stained eyes.

"Yes, but she's poorly."

Davy was silent for a moment, watching her moving fingers.

"Is she too poorly to see me?"

"It depends what you want," the child replied, with some spirit.

"A man came yesterday who frightened her – he was rough and rude. She has much to bear at present, and I'm not to let anyone in today."

Davy digested this piece of information. He felt his brain sludging through the fog – he wished he were quick-witted like his master. He realised that the man, whoever he was, had not brought the brother with him. He was still missing then, - or was he inside?

"I am come to find a missing belt," he told her, "Ben Glover, who died in the Abbey before your sister, was my friend. His wife has missed a belt she gave him as a gift – she hoped Mistress Fosse might have returned it with Mary's goods in error."

Her lips trembled at the mention of Mary.

"It's because of Mary – and now Roger – that mother is unwell," she told him, pausing in her work."

"Is your brother here?" Davy asked, "Perhaps he could look for me?"

Mary shook her head.

"Roger hasn't come home since two days," she answered, with a catch in her voice.

"Mother thinks he's off thieving again, and that frightens her. He could be hanged, you know, if he's caught."

"Why does she think he's thieving?" Davy asked.

"Because he's done it before. Father beat him, but it didn't stop him. The man who came yesterday said he'd stolen something from him, and made mother let him search his room. He even made mother fetch Mary's things in case he had hidden it there. Roger might, too. He's a clever thief."

So the men had not brought Roger home with them then – where had they taken him, Davy wondered, uneasily.

A shadow passed over the doorway. Davy turned to see the young priest.

"Father Peter helped us yesterday," she said, greeting him with some relief.

"He went up with the man and stood over him to make sure he did not steal from us."

"He was an unfeeling and arrogant man," Father Peter declared. "He did not find whatever he was looking for."

His young face expressed concern for the family, and he looked sternly towards Davy.

"The family in this cottage is in much need of rest and prayer," he said, "let me have concern for this belt. I know where to find you should it be found when Johanna is well enough to search. She seems overcome with weariness and despair just now."

Davy thanked him and told him where to find Lydia. His face darkened when he heard of the fire and the loss of her house.

"This is a sad affair," he mused, "and how did these two young people become involved?"

Davy had no answer for that, and after one or two more civilities with the priest, he took his leave, feeling somehow foolish and patronised.

On his way home, Davy could not help but think how little information he had discovered – except the fact that the boy Roger had not returned home and appeared to be missing.

The robed watcher smiled as Davy rejoined the trackway to Milborne Port. How easy it was to discover the players in this drama! He could plot their movements so easily!

Abbot Bradford made every effort to appear hospitable to Sir Tobias. The two men met in the Abbot's house, and refreshed by fine wine, Sir Tobias was able to look out of the glassed windows onto the Abbey garden. The swelling buds on the bare trees promised a Spring in the not too distant future, fresh green shoots appearing delicately in the orchard garden.

"You have many lay workers in the monastery," Sir Tobias began. The Abbot inclined his head graciously, and pressed his finger tips together, elbows on the wooden arms of his chair.

"Do you know all of them personally?"

The Abbot allowed himself a small laugh.

"No, my lord Coroner. Many of them I know by sight – some of them I know by name, but all are known to the brother in charge of their particular area of work."

"Then I have quite a task in front of me," said Sir Tobias, drily. The Abbot looked startled.

"Surely you don't intend questioning them all?" he asked.

"Abbot Bradford, two young people were murdered within your Abbey grounds – one of them actually in the Lady Chapel. The widow of one of them has had her house fired by two men who appeared to be monks. Can you really expect me not to question?" Sir Tobias looked thunderous. Abbot Bradford tried to back-track.

"Her house fired? I did not know that," he purred

"Neither did I, until my young friend the would-be schoolmaster of Milborne Port rode into my courtyard with the news. Now – tell me – how many monks reside here – and how many lay persons do you have in your employ?"

The Abbot sighed and rose to his feet, selecting a key from the jangle of keys on his belt.

"I will fetch Prior Simon and our register and account books," he said, a note of resignation in his voice.

Sir Tobias leaned back in his chair to wait. The room was pleasant, full of morning light, and the view of the Abbey garden was uninterrupted. The Abbot's wine was smooth; the wooden floor was polished and smelt of beeswax; a crucifix hung on the wall behind the table on which was a heavy book.

Sir Tobias reflected on the news that Matthias had brought. It certainly gave the incidents a graver, more sinister picture. Who would fire the house of a woman so recently widowed – and so recently in child-birth? This action, more than the two deaths, had fired Sir Tobias' resolve. Had not his own daughter been in child-birth just a few years ago? How vulnerable she had been immediately after the birth – how weak and tearful – how open to all suggestions, swayed by any little idea – clutching at straws to find a direction in which to go when she was not suckling her new little boy. Sir Tobias' face softened. The boy Luke – a grandson – yes, definitely a candidate for Thomas Copeland.

He had left Matthias with the Lady Bridget in his own home, and had ridden to the Abbot, his sense of justice fully roused, and was here with particular regard to the two monks seen at Lydia's, and again at the house of Mistress Fosse.

Abbot Bradford returned with Prior Simon, carrying his register and accounting books.

"So – it appears you have twentyfour monks at present, including your two selves," growled Sir Tobias, after consulting the lists.

"Plus seven infirmarians," added Prior Simon.

"And all of these are long-standing? You have no new admissions? No new novitiates?"

No, it appeared not. Holy orders were losing popularity in the beginning of this new age.

"I will need to see them all," Sir Tobias announced, firmly.

The Abbot shook his head in disbelief. How like the Northern part of Dorset to find themselves with an honest coroner, who ferreted after the truth! He tried one last approach, as tactfully and as guilelessly as he was able.

"My Lord Coroner, Your young grandson might perhaps wish to study in the future – on a scholarship provided perhaps by the Abbey....?"

The question hung in the air – Prior Simon held his breath in the lull before the tempest.

Sir Tobias let forth his fullest throated roar, and turned to face Abbot Bradford.

"We are not discussing my grandson's schooling, for which I shall pay," he bellowed, "we are investigating the cruel deaths of two of someone's flock – deaths which happened in your hundred, in your abbey...and as a consequence of these deaths, a young widow's house was burned to the ground. She and her newborn daughter would have been inside were it not for the quick thinking of Matthias Barton. Then your holy church would have had four deaths at its door – and you speak to me of scholarships for my grandson? How dare you, Abbot Bradford, how dare you!"

It was good to see the proud and haughty Abbot flinch under the tirade, Prior Simon thought, and then mentally flagellated himself for indulging in such delicious malice. He opened the accounts book as if nothing had happened.

"You misunderstand me –" the Abbot began,

"I think not," rejoined Sir Tobias, crisply.

"As you wish, my Lord Coroner," returned the other, pressing his thin lips together as if offended by being so misunderstood. He was right – North Dorset did indeed have an honest coroner who would seek out wrong doers until they were justly punished. Despite the rebuke for his implied bribe, he felt a shaft of sneaking admiration for the man.

Prior Simon sat down with Sir Tobias, and together they ran their eye over the list of paid employees of the monastery, - all lay people from the town or its surrounds.

"You have over fifty men and women to look after just twenty four monks?" Sir Tobias asked with some disdain.

"The brother's task is to pray," Abbot Bradford reminded him, frostily, "They cannot be expected to work twentyfour hours a day and pray twenty-four hours a day."

"But why vintners, bakers, carpenters, pot boys, stable lads, gardeners, serving girls – the list is endless," Sir Tobias said.

Prior Simon glanced up slyly.

"Surely you will not expect to speak to all these then, my Lord Coroner? It will take many hours."

Father Abbot shot him an approving glance.

"I will start with yourself and your brothers," Sir Tobias decided. "Then if necessary, I will request help from Matthias Barton, with your permission."

"That is irregular," Abbot Bradford said at once. "Matthias Barton, as you yourself said, is a young man of Milborne Port. He is not a Sherborne man. I have a bailiff who will be pleased to assist you."

"Very well," Sir Tobias agreed resignedly. He knew he had no choice in the matter.

"But I would like to speak first to the brother who prayed in AllHallows with the young man's body."

Abbot Bradford glanced at Prior Simon for a name. Prior Simon stared blankly back.

"There was no brother detailed to remain in the chapel" Prior Simon said

"I think you are mistaken, Sir Tobias

The young man's friend visited the chapel..." he said, with a puzzled frown,

"There was a brother in attendance on the body."

"With respect, Sir Tobias, there was not." Prior Simon spoke with authority

on this point.

"Strange," mused Sir Tobias, "I believe there was a person in Benedictine garb in the chapel. However, it may have been one of your more compassionate brothers giving of his own time?"

Abbot Bradford noted the barb and smouldered.

Sir Tobias was forced to concede that this was so, and be pleased to accept the Abbot's bailiff.

The Abbot called in his scribe, who by the gleam in his eye and the satisfied smirk on his face, had heard most of the conversation by simply pressing his ear to the door.

Abbot Bradford was not able to offer any further help. He had prayed on the night of Ben's murder. How did he know? Because he prayed every night after offices had been sung in the monastery chapel. Had he been present at the final office of the day? Evasive – he could not be certain. Sir Tobias suspected he was not always present at offices sung at inhospitable times. Had the Lady Chapel been re-consecrated? Yes, it had. Who was present? Himself, Prior Simon, Father Samuel, - and as many of the brothers as wished to be present. How many was that? He didn't know. Were there any lay people present? No. How often did the brothers leave the vicinity of the monastery and abbey church? Several of them at various times walked in the immediate environs of the town for diverse reasons, but on the whole, the monastery was their world. They had everything they needed. And a lot more besides, Sir Tobias thought, in disgust. It was becoming clear that the brothers led a fairly easy life, and that Abbot Bradford was far removed from the life of the town.

"The argument you had with Father Samuel," began Sir Tobias, trying a new tack,

"Correction, Sir Tobias," interrupted Abbot Bradford, "The argument is not of my making. The argument lies with Father Samuel." The scribe raised his eyes to his master's face, expecting another explosion, but Sir Tobias' face was calm and serene.

"Quite so," he remarked, "Might it throw any light on our present matter? I understand there are some very angry people in the town at present."

"Their anger is a storm in a piss-pot," expostulated the Abbot.

"I have narrowed an archway and they have built their own font in the Chapel of Ease – entirely unsuitable, and, if I may say so, illegal. They are being fanned into rash words and actions by the very man I appointed as priest-in-charge of All Hallows, - which is only a chapel of ease. St. Mary the virgin – our Abbey church – is the mother church – and they know that it is. But no – although the topic is becoming a festering boil, it cannot be a killing matter. Until this first death, I knew nothing of this apprentice. He did not worship with Father Samuel, he was nearing the end of his apprenticeship and was, so I understand, preparing to go back to Milborne Port to live."

Sir Tobias was amazed at the venom and bitterness which had spewed out of the Holy Abbot as he spoke of the quarrel.

Here was surely a man who would be obeyed....a proud man who could not forgive a slight...but he was right. This was a town concern and although town factions were not wholly united against the Abbot, and the sore was spreading as Easter approached, it could hardly be a killing matter.

He spent the rest of the day with the brothers, his scribe enjoying every moment of his insight into the holy places where so much luxury seemed to lie. He spoke finally with Brother Francis, who had duties in the infirmary, and so he came to him last, after he had spoken somewhat more gently and kindly to the seven elderly brothers who were seeing out the end of their days here.

Brother Francis was himself elderly, but certainly not infirm. He did remember seeing two shadowy figures in the garden when he had risen to ease his digestive processes.

Didn't he think it strange? Yes, he admitted, a little bashfully, but he'd assumed it to be younger brothers slipping back into the dorter after a night in the town whore house. This did not surprise Sir Tobias – rather it saddened him as an admission of the changing face of the church. Had he any idea of whom it might be? Here, Brother Francis had paused. He had no real idea, but there were three or four brothers who might well fall into that category, - but no, he couldn't say for sure. Had he not thought of glancing at the dorter to see whether there were empty beds? No, sadly he had not.

There seemed little else the brothers could tell him so Sir Tobias went down to the guesten hall to speak with the chamberlain monk.

Documentation here was slack. The guesten hall was mostly run by lay persons, few of whom could read or write, and Brother Jerome did not keep a written record of travellers.

"On some days – fair days – there are too many of them," he said.

Sir Tobias tried to jog his memory,

"The day before yesterday", he said, "A young well-made man with auburn hair,.. He would have been tired and wet through." He waited hopefully.

"Yes, yes – he sat on that bench-" he indicated the high-backed bench on which Matthias had sat. "Phoebe would have served him"

Sir Tobias wearily tried Phoebe.

"The weather worsened during the afternoon, sir," she told him, nervously. "There were several travellers in after the red-haired gentleman. He left before dark, I remember."

"What can you remember about the other travellers, Phoebe?" he asked, gently. She was slow and middle-aged, her hair neatly tucked into a cap, and a large, clean white apron covering her russet dress. She wrinkled her face into a concentrated frown.

"There were two merchants ,- I do remember they – been in here afore, they have, – they were wet through, too. They left just after the red-haired man. Wanted to get somewhere afore dark I suppose."

"Good," encouraged Sir Tobias. He had Matthias description of the two in whom he was interested, but he wanted to hear it from someone else as well.

"There was a sea captain from Poole – He had business in town he did say."

Sir Tobias waited. Phoebe closed her eyes, the better to picture the afternoon in question.

"The two merchants sat behind the young man – I think they carry spices or something like. They did converse with a monk, but he was not one of ours. They spoke with him a little while."

"Have the fine spice merchants gone now? Sir Tobias asked.

"Oh, yes, sir. I told you – they left soon after the other gentleman."

Sir Tobias had to be content with that – it was the only information he could establish from his visit. Was the monk seen briefly with them the same one who had prayed – or watched- in the chapel? He thought it probably was, and he thought the idea of prayer was nonsense. Presumably the monk had been asked, or even ordered, to stay close to the body to see who came to see, to lead them to any family or friends in whom Ben might have confided.

He outlined his meagre findings to William that evening. Matthias had long left for his own home, and Lady Bridget and her husband were enjoying peace together before retiring.

"Do you think the merchants are significant?" Sir Tobias mused, frowning in the shadows of their comfortable room.

"It would seem they may be – could the monastery's guesten house be a meeting place for messages? What would a sea captain from Poole be doing so far from home?" the Lady Bridget wondered. "And how does the unknown Benedictine fit in? Is he from the Abbey?"

William's round face creased in concern. He was a little younger than Sir Tobias, - a fighting man who had followed Sir Tobias through France as his squire, and who had seen death at the hands of the French - and French dead, too. He'd experienced plunder, seen rape victims, heard the screams of women as they were dragged from their houses – even from their churches. He had been pleased when Sir Tobias had been wounded sufficiently to return home to Dorset, where Lady Bridget and William had refused to allow Sir Tobias to give up and die.

William remembered well how he'd had to leave Sir Tobias, half conscious, on the quay side at Calais, propped against a bale of rope. The binding of his wound, which had been a deep gash to the bone in one thigh, and a head wound which William felt wholly responsible for, had been attended to in a nunnery, but was opening again due to the movement of the destrier. He had lashed Sir Tobias to the high war saddle of his destrier and led him to Calais – two days it had taken, and the countryside unfriendly, sullen, deserted, blackened. They had travelled by night. At Calais he'd paid for their passage by selling the destrier. How he'd dreaded having to tell Sir Tobias that on his recovery! A destrier cost many marks of silver, but William had nothing else of value to sell. The armour had been damaged in battle – the removal of the helmet by William had cost Sir Tobias his head wound from a stray arrow, and what was left of the armour he had used to pay for his medicines in the nunnery. Besides that, armour was too heavy to transport when a man's life hung in the balance, so William had travelled light. He'd sold Sir Tobias' gold ring at Poole to pay for the hire of a horse to get them home, and three days later, with Sir Tobias still semi-conscious and near to death, he'd led the horse into Purse Caundle. Once there, he and the Lady Bridget had simply refused to allow him to die.

"I will go to the coast and enquire regarding this sea captain," he said. "These men could be French spies."

"There is very little to spy on in our corner of Dorset," Sir Tobias reminded him, "but yes, - go. Poole is probably our biggest harbour now. It may be rather tenuous, but it seems our only lead."

Sir Tobias and Lady Bridget retired to their private solar, and William prepared himself for yet another journey. He did not mind – he was restless by nature and enjoyed travelling. His life was bound to Sir Tobias and he was content that it was so.

Chapter 9

Matthias Barton was restless. He had ridden hard home from Purse Caundle, arriving at Barton Holding as daylight faded, and now at the end of his solitary meal, found himself restless and dissatisfied again. The Lady Bridget had given him food to break his fast after his early morning ride. He had spoken with Sir Tobias at length, and had felt a surge of relief as the coroner's face had darkened and he'd called for his scribe to accompany him to Sherborne.

"Your task is to watch, Matthias," he had said, as the horse clattered on the cobbles in the courtyard. His scribe slung his satchel with writing tools and vellums over his shoulder and mounted his fat little pony. William, armed as usual to provide safety on the road, brought up the rear, and the little trio were soon gone. Matthias would have liked to have gone with them, but as well as watch, Sir Tobias had also expressed concern for the missing boy.

"Watch out for the boy, if you can," he said, "do nothing to cause these men alarm – just watch."

Matthias had lingered in the garden with Lady Bridget long enough to hear horses hooves in the courtyard. Alice and Luke had ridden from their home, and Matthias found he was disturbed by Alice's presence. It was difficult not to be rude when Lady Bridget invited him to take warm spiced wine with them before he left. He hoped he had not appeared sullen as he accepted.

Luke was taken outside to see a litter of kittens newly born, and for a few minutes Matthias was alone with Alice. Conversation was stilted. Alice had expected her father to be there, and instead there was Matthias, whom she did not know. Matthias was not certain how much he should say about his business with Sir Tobias, and he was discomfited that although he had two sisters and been most comfortable in their presence, he was tongue-tied and embarrassed simply at being in the room with her.

He stayed only as long as courtesy dictated, and was relieved to be away from the house. As he left, he heard Alice laugh – a rich sound, filling his ears with a merry sound. He hoped she was not laughing at him.

Now, as he sat alone in his own solar, he envied Davy and Elizabeth their married state – and Alice and whatever her husband was called. He could see the comfortable ease which existed between Sir Tobias and Lady Bridget, and he remembered the firm feeling of security he'd had as a boy, when, repast over, his mother and father would exchange glances and retire to their own rooms. He could appreciate the depth of grief and loneliness Lydia must feel – and her fear, too, at facing an uncertain future.

He couldn't help his mind dwelling on Alice – her proud, uplifted breasts, her trim waist with its girdle tightly pulled in, which accentuated those firm breasts, rounded and feminine. Her hair had been fastened into two plaits and braided to match her girdle. One of the plaits lay on those tempting breasts, and he imagined them rising and falling with her uneven breath as he cupped his hands round them. Her skin would be soft and smooth to touch, and to unbraid her hair would be an erotic luxury, candle light glistening on her milk white skin. He felt a pleasant stirring in his loins and lingered to enjoy the sensation - he stroked her back and found the fastenings of her gown. His body moved in a gentle thrust without him being aware of it.... for a few moments he was only conscious of the delightful and exciting sensation of a new sexual awakening that had died when his family had been destroyed. He closed his eyes and allowed his senses to take control of his imagination.

His pleasure was short lived and unfulfilled. He sat up in self-disgust. However would he face Alice again after such delicious and lascivious thoughts? She was a married woman with a child of her own, and she the daughter of a man he admired. And yet the feeling remained – a physical ache that had been awakened and now increased his restlessness and sense of dissatisfaction with his life.

His sense of loneliness remained physical as he retired to bed, and for the first time since returning from Italy, he yearned for the vibrant colour, warmth and vulgarity of the foreign whore houses. A man could be roused with lust and buy a night's satisfaction there, and face the next day with pride in the performance.

Perhaps he had been wrong to return to this little backwater, with only Davy and Elizabeth for company? He thought he was done with restless travel.

The following day he had a genuine need to go down into Sherborne to place an order for cloth. He tried to concentrate on his own business, and Davy had set trestles and wooden benches in the room leading off the open main hall where the fire burned warmly. He had obtained inks, quills and horn books and immediately after the feast of Easter, his first five pupils would begin.

They would start at eight in the morning, pause for a simple repast at midday, and leave before sunset. During Winter months this would be about three in the afternoon. All five boys were to come daily, for Matthias had not considered himself established enough to offer them board. Three boys were from Milborne Port, and two from outlying manors. All families were merchants who had made progress in this changing world; they could see the value of their sons being able to read, write, do simple accounts and learn something of the wider world in order to increase their trade and social standing. Matthew would need to provide stabling or grazing for their ponies during the day. Davy's job was to attend to that.

He thought of the tapestries and hangings in Lady Bridget's home as he trotted briskly down Pig Hill, past the castle and so into Long Street. He needed to visit the cloth merchant for suitable hangings for his hall, lest the five boys gave him no privacy during the day. Davy and Elizabeth's living arrangements must not be disturbed, and his high hall was large enough to take some simple hangings to avoid the boys being forever in his sight during their day.

The business in the market was brisk. The sight of the busy stalls mended Matthias' good humour to a degree. The colour and chatter of the market place restored his feeling of purpose and he found himself exchanging pleasantries with fellow customers. There was always noise in the market place..street cries, itinerant entertainers hoping for coins and dogs and children dodging in and out of shop fronts and stalls. Matthias paused to smile at a dog fight between two dogs with the same stolen bone, their owners calling them frantically as they caused mayhem amongst the crowded street.

He dawdled at the cloth merchant's stall, uncertain of what to buy. He would have liked to have asked the Lady Bridget's advice, but the connection was too tenuous. There was some Salisbury cloth available today, its distinctive dyed stripes making a cheery statement, but eventually Matthias chose some locally dyed dark red cloth for heavier hangings. He parted with what seemed to him an extortionate amount of coin, ruefully aware that in the past his mother would have encouraged him to question the price and quality.

A crowd had gathered at the edge of the market, and aware of Sir Tobias' instruction to him to watch, Matthias wandered over, the cloth heavy in his arms. The Abbey gatehouse was thronged with townspeople, jostling and muttering angrily. Matthias joined the crowd, and craned his neck over the people to attempt to see the cause.

Father Samuel was at the front of the crowd, standing on the steps of the almonry.

"This is a disgrace!" he shouted, his voice reaching clearly to Matthias, who stood at the back of the crowd. Clutching his cloth awkwardly, he tried to push further forward to see better.

"Look how little food has been put out for the poor! And this Abbey is a rich abbey! Where is the charity we have a right to expect?"

The crowd murmured its agreement, and Matthias pushed through to the front, where he could see the steps leading to the almonry. The door was closed. There were a handful of beggars fighting over a basket of bread, seemingly oblivious of Father Samuel.

"I shall demand an audience with Abbot Bradford!" Father Samuel announced. "Those who would be numbered amongst the complainants, follow me! This is no act of charity – this is scandalous!"

Half the crowd followed him through the lane and onto the Abbey green, where the building work was still progressing apace.

"These masons and their labourers are taking liberties with our church," Father Samuel shouted. "At Easter, we need to see a clear nave, - not all this building rubbish. Have some reverence for the great work you're doing," he shouted up at the working men. They waved to him from their perches on the scaffolding. Matthias thought it unlikely they'd heard what he said.

There were some townspeople left by the almonry steps. The last beggars had emptied the basket and scuttled away with their meagre pickings.

"Father Samuel is too hot," the butcher, Walter Gallor, declared. "Much of what he says is true. This is a disgrace – the good brothers have plenty of waste food. Not enough appears here for the poor, but little will be gained by antagonizing Abbot Bradford. He is the Abbot. Whatever he decrees should be regarded. I cannot agree with the spittle Father Samuel produces."

"I warrant the Easter procession will not be as good as usual, Walter," Thomas Twogood commented. His trade was slack on this day, and he was undecided whether to support Father Samuel or the moderates.

The miller grunted, and turned back to collect his cart.

"It doesn't do to stir up trouble,' he warned. "Abbot Bradford is a powerful man. Look how he takes port-rent from you all. We can do nothing in this town without the Abbot's say-so, and if not the Abbot, then the Bishop of Salisbury. They've got us all nicely tied up."

Walter Gallor watched his retreating back.

"Daniel couldn't be more right," he observed. "The Abbot owns Daniel's mill – Daniel pays him rent. The Abbot owns the market, We pay him port-rent. The Bishop even taxes the brewers – they still have to pay him croukpenny. The church has got it tied up nicely. But I still don't like to oppose the Father Abbot – we need to be reasonable."

Matthias drifted away. There was nothing to be learned here, except town dissent. He wondered what would happen on Easter Sunday, when the townspeople tried to enter the Abbey church through the narrowed doorway, with their crosses and banners. It might be worth going down to Sherborne on Easter Sunday to mass to see what happened rather than hearing mass in Milborne Port as he usually did.

He reclaimed his horse and laid the cloth across the front of his saddle. He should have brought Davy with him to carry his purchases, but this would have to do.

He retraced his steps down Long Street and then, mentally flattened by his lack of activity, turned the horse towards Newland, where he'd last seen Roger. This took him up Cheap Street, past Thomas Copeland's house and then swung him into Hound Street, where Mistress Fosse lived. He passed her house, but there was no sign of life there, - and climbed the hill towards

Newland. It was here he'd last seen the lad. He'd lost him by the ale house.

It was a trail gone cold – not that it had been much of a trail in the first place. Matthias felt he could waste no more time, and trotted towards Castleton Mill to join the track to Shaftesbury.

He arrived at Barton Holding feeling he'd used his time badly. Davy had reached home before him, in despondent mood also.

"We're getting nowhere, Master," he said, gloomily. "No sign of the lad – I'm not the right person to ferret out information. My mind just doesn't work quickly enough to sound convincing."

He set Matthias' meal on the table, topped his goblet up with ale, stoked the fire and left Matthias in peace to eat.

The shadows flickered on the walls of the high roofed hall. The candles were lit and mellowed the surrounding room, soft light filling the corners. Beeswax candles were one of Matthias' few luxuries – tallow candles smoked too much and smelt unpleasant.

"One day," thought Matthias, as he took his knife out to start his meal, "One day I could build above this hall – make an upstairs sleeping room.....maybe more than one, if I ever have a wife and children."

His thoughts turned once more to Alice – trim and lively , sweet of face, and gentle towards her little son.... he wondered glumly what chance he had of finding a suitable wife. He imagined Alice presiding calmly over her household – husband – child – serving girl – serving man for her husband – what did her husband do? – and in due course, another child on the way....making plans for her garden possibly – herbs to be planted

– maybe she and her husband had a little land, and they'd plant a rose garden and a lavender bed.. some medicinal herbs – possibly they'd add to their home as the children kept coming....would Luke go to school in Sherborne?

Without brothers and sisters, parents, companions around him, how could he expect to meet anyone suitable? It would have been so easy if his sisters had lived.....their friends.... their acquaintances.... daughters of his mother's friends.....

A shout of alarm cut across his thoughts. Doors banged and Davy's voice calling brought him to his feet.

"Out the back, Master Barton! Intruders!"

Matthias followed Davy out of the door, across the cobbled courtyard and into the darkness beyond. He saw Davy's shadow crumple as he drew level with the box hedge and heard his shriek of pain.

Instinctively he drew back a few paces and jumped onto the low wall which ran beside the hedge. He heard the rustle of leaves under softly clad feet and hoped Davy wasn't too badly hurt. Whoever the intruder was, he was waiting for Matthias to appear at the other end of the hedge.. Matthias kept still, peering through the thickly twigged hedge. His eyes grew accustomed to the dark, and he could hear Davy's heavy, shuddering breathing. He could dimly make out the shape of a man standing the other side of the hedge, tensed for attack. Without stopping to consider the consequences, Matthias ran lightly over the wall and round the hedge so that he was behind the tensed figure, and before the man could turn to see the cause of the flurry behind him, Matthias, from his slightly elevated position on the wall, leapt onto the attacker's back and wound his legs round his waist, raining blows on his head with his two clenched fists.

His attacker whirled round, snarling and punching back, lashing out in the dark. One hand held a glittering knife, and the violence of Matthias' blows raining on his head caused him to drop this, making a clatter on the cobbles, although not before he had caught Matthias' arm, slicing him down his forearm. Davy, groaning in pain but the breath now returning to him, rolled over onto the knife, and with a quick sideways movement, the attacker was gone, leaping over the gate into the paddock, and before either men could give chase, they heard the thud of hooves as the man mounted his waiting horse and was off.

"Up, Davy – quick!" gasped Matthias.

Davy staggered up, shuddering with a winded gullet. "Over there, Master!"

"A large horse- the same as when Lydia's house was fired!" Matthias panted.

"We'll never catch him!" Davy groaned, clutching the gate post and lowering himself down to the ground again.

"I'm bleeding," Matthias said in some surprise, as he felt the hot, sticky fluid run down his arm and soak into his tunic.

Pressing his good hand against his bleeding arm, Matthias ran to the gate, but he was too late, - in the weak moonlight he could see the horseman, dark-cloaked and hooded, bending low over his steed, swerving round a clump of bushes and so on to the track. It wasn't even possible to ascertain whether he was bound for Shaftesbury or Sherborne, but Matthias guessed Sherborne.

Elizabeth's frightened voice called to them from the door – she stood there holding a guttering candle, and in its weak light, Davy hauled himself onto his knees and leaning hard on the little wall, eased himself up, breathing laboriously. He paused to rest, his breath coming unevenly. Matthias moved into the circle of light and Elizabeth gave a cry of concern as she saw his arm, sliced down the inside from shoulder to wrist.

With his good side, Matthias supported Davy, and together they re-entered the house. Elizabeth, practical in emergency, and with a little knowledge of herbal remedies, administered to both of them. Davy was badly winded. He remained sitting in front of the fire for some time, grey faced, shuddering and retching, his breath coming in shallow gasps. As he began to recover his senses, he was aware that every time he breathed in, a knife-like pain attacked the bottom of his rib cage. Elizabeth felt carefully with her fingers, but Davy couldn't stand the pain of their probing, however gentle she tried to be. She propped him up in front of the fire with the sheepskin tucked round him. He found if he stayed very still and breathed very carefully, he could stand the pain, and so he stayed, until morning broke.

Matthias' sliced arm was easier to deal with. The attacker had been caught by surprise, and the cut was superficial, although it had bled copiously to start with. Cloths, torn in pieces and administered tightly, soon stemmed the flow, and Matthias slumped in Elizabeth's other chair in the kitchen, his own bed forgotten, as he dreamed uneasily of hedges, shadows and mounted monks. His sleep was shallow. Every so often he would wake and find himself shaking with shock and listening for any sound. All he could hear was Davy's broken breathing, and owls hooting softly outside.

In the morning he felt as though he was drowning in a morass of half truths, hidden meanings and muddle.

Chapter 10

Matthias knew he must visit Purse Caundle with some urgency. Davy appeared to have a broken rib for breathing hurt him, and he himself had a sore arm which would not bear much movement. He sat in the cold grey light of late March and watched Elizabeth kindle a flame in the fire.

"What's to be done, Elizabeth?" he asked. He was not in the habit of asking her for advice, but Davy was still sleeping uneasily, and Matthias felt a need to share his thoughts. Elizabeth had been steady and quick in her actions after the intruder had left, and Matthias was grateful for her presence. They had the kitchen to themselves, for Lydia had returned to her mother's house with the babe.

Elizabeth sat back on her heels as she stirred the ashes.

"This thing needs to be treated more seriously than you thought, sir," she ventured, blushing pink as she realised her opinion was being sought.

"As you said last evening, you have brushed against something deeper than you realised. Ben's death was the beginning, but there seems to be no end, and it needs taking seriously."

"Am I not taking it seriously?" Matthias asked, leaning forward in his chair. Elizabeth frowned with concentration as she tried to express her thoughts clearly without being thought critical of her master.

"You have dabbled, sir. You went with Davy to see Ben's body. You tried to see the coroner after Mary died – Lydia's house was fired, but you left too much time between that happening and informing the coroner. Davy went to Oborne and asked questions and now the young lad has disappeared.....it's all such a slow moving muddle. We live in such a quiet little corner that it's difficult to imagine king's spies or foreign agents here."

Matthias was startled into total wakefulness. How did Elizabeth – a woman – know about the king's very comprehensive spy ring? And what made her mention foreign agents? Matthias' mind had dwelled more on theft or blackmail. He paused so long before speaking again that Elizabeth was afraid she had said too much.

"What do you know about spy rings?" he asked her eventually.

"Very little sir," was the demure reply, "but your father knew of such things, and once said he was glad to be out of them."

Matthias felt his jaw slacken with amazement. His father? From Elizabeth's words it appeared that perhaps his father had once been involved in such service to the king.

"I'm only repeating what I heard," she added hastily, "and I know the King has informers everywhere."

Yes, Matthias knew that, too, but not here, not in Milborne Port – and for what purpose? Or even Sherborne, - the Abbey was large and beautiful and yielded much revenue to the Bishop of Salisbury, but Sherborne was small and insignificant compared to Shaftesbury, where the good nuns had their well ordered stronghold – and there was Glastonbury – and Exeter. No – King's spies – certainly not. But foreign agents?

England was still at war with France, although losing heavily now. Already, disillusioned soldiers who had not been paid were beginning to desert and filter back to England through the South Coast ports. Sir Tobias had spoken of them the other day – hungry, cold, diseased – they would tramp from their destinations without a lord to serve, and needing food and shelter. They would be lawless and desperate men who must rob and plunder to stay alive. Surely with England on the losing side now, and with little more than a boy king, there was no need for French spies? But the machinations of the great lords of the land were sowing dissent and disharmony as the young Henry struggled to live up to his father..... and my Lord Suffolk held a grip of power...Matthias thanked God for the remoteness of their lives, here in Dorset. How would the great lords of the land resolve things if the young king failed to prove strong?

But she had sown the seed in his mind, and he needed more than ever to speak with Sir Tobias.

He dozed fitfully again before the re-kindled fire, and woke when Elizabeth had prepared some oatmeal for them all.

"I must ride to Purse Caundle, Elizabeth, if you will dress my arm again for me. We need help from Sir Tobias. My confused interference in this has put my household in danger, but I don't understand why."

He ate his oatmeal in silence, cursing himself for his sloth in delaying carrying the news of the fired roof to Sir Tobias, and with Davy still sleeping, he allowed Elizabeth to re-dress his arm, binding it as tightly as he could bear.

She had to assist him to pull his sur-cotte and woollen over-cloak on securely, and to his shame, it was

Elizabeth who saddled his horse and helped him to mount. He sheathed his father's best dagger in his belt, and tucked his own smaller fine -bladed knife inside his cloak.

The sun was bright now, casting aside the shadowy nightmare, and as Matthias turned his horse out of Milborne Port onto the Shaftesbury track, he hoped to be able to shed some light on their predicament so they could return to normality, and his dreams of a peaceful, scholarly existence.

He did not ride fast, as every pothole and mudslide jarred his arm, and he passed several parties of pedlars, chapmen and other traders making for Sherborne to peddle their wares in the approach to Easter.

Outside Milborne Port, the Bishop's great hunting forest began, offering a short cut to Purse Caundle, but Matthias had no stomach for it today. He kept strictly to the edge of the forest, finally turning towards the South, leaving the main track and taking the smaller one towards Purse Caundle. He did not see the solitary figure following him at a distance – and being still inexperienced in the matter of murder, it did not occur to him to even think that he might be followed. As he reached Sir Tobias' house and turned in, the mounted watcher turned back; he had his answer – Matthias was visiting the coroner.

Sir Tobias and his scribe were sifting through recent cases prior to relegating them to the great wooden chest when Lady Bridget greeted Matthias. She made an exclamation of concern as Matthias dismounted, slithering down with less grace and expertise then normal, and staggering slightly to regain his balance.

"Matthias! Welcome! You're hurt?"

"Mild compared to my man Davy," Matthias assured her, handing his reins to the boy who had come running out from the stable.

"Have you been attacked?" the Lady Bridget asked, taking hold of Matthias' swaddled arm.

"In my own home – an intruder," Matthias explained.

Lady Bridget wasted no time in taking him to the airy room looking out over the garden, where Sir Tobias and his scribe Nicholas were doing their work.

"Matthias!" Sir Tobias said, rising to his feet. "Something serious brings you here?"

Matthias was surprised at how relieved he was to be able to sit in a chair that didn't bounce and move. He rested his arm across his chest, and explained the happenings of the night to Sir Tobias.

"I seem to have become involved in something that has put my household at risk," he finished, "and I perhaps have not taken things seriously enough. I've allowed Davy to investigate without due concern for who might notice – I've wasted several days in self doubt and depression, and it's blown my plans off course. So,- now what's to be done?"

Sir Tobias rested his chin on his hands, elbows on the table in front of him. Nicholas put the parchment to one side and laid down his quill.

"I'm waiting for William to return from Poole," Sir Tobias began, "There was a sea-captain in the monastery when you rested there. Two of the men whom you over-heard were on hired horses which the stable boy thought came from Poole – and Poole is, as you know, a sea port with access to France."

"The King's spy network is in a degree of confusion," Sir Tobias continued, reluctantly. "He comes of age, as you know, Matthias, this year, and there is great rivalry in court between those who have been his regents and protectors.....but Sherborne is too small and insignificant to be involved in serious King's business. We must look to the Abbey, despite the possible connection to France through Poole, - and we must look fast, for the boy is still missing."

Matthias furrowed his brow and gnawed on his lip.

"Ben was apprenticed to Richard Cope. When I asked about customers he'd visited for Master Cope, the merchant refused to tell me. He was evasive – and I didn't follow that up – I didn't really have any authority to do so, in any case.

"So it's possible that Richard Cope might know something of value. I doubt he's directly involved – he's too canny to dirty his hands, but I shall call on him and press him for information," decided Sir Tobias.

Matthias tried to organize his thoughts.

"We haven't traced the source of the coins, - nor do we know for what they were searching. Mary was killed in the same way as Ben, so we can assume it to be the same person. Why would Ben involve Mary?"

Sir Tobias sat up suddenly.

"Maybe that's the wrong way round, Matthias. Maybe Mary involved Ben."

"So that takes us back further – to her brother Roger," Matthias mused.

"Brother Roger is a young and skilled thief, apparently.The little sister told Davy that Roger had been stealing again – the searcher at the house was convinced Roger had stolen something."

"Who were they stealing for?" Sir Tobias rumbled. He rubbed his hands through his hair in frustration. 'And what was it that he stole?

"How did anyone know of my involvement?" Matthias wondered, troubled suddenly at leaving Davy and Elizabeth alone for too long.

"Who knew you were enquiring? Tell me, Matthias." Matthias forced his brain to work.

"Mistress Fosse, - Davy went to look for Ben, and she knew Davy worked for me, but that's too tenuous to be worthwhile. Richard Cope, the glover – he was indignant that I asked for the names of customers Ben had visited. The Abbot himself and Prior Simon..... Lydia and her mother – highly unlikely.......Mary's family.....and I suppose the young priest who helped Davy when I sent him to Mary's home....all very unlikely ..." he tailed off uncertainly.

"Were you seen when you frightened off the men who fired Lydia's roof?" Sir Tobias asked sudden "It's possible," Matthias admitted, "although it was dark, there was light from the flames which burned up very quickly, - and I jumped right out of hiding to throw stones at the horses."

"You may well have been seen, and then recognized afterwards. Have you been followed?"

"Followed?" Matthias asked bleakly, "I really have no idea. It simply didn't occur to me."

A chill came over him. What purpose could there possibly be in following him? He said so to Sir Tobias.

"You are surprisingly naïve, Matthias. There is a rich prize here somewhere, - if we can discover its origin. You may have been a marked man from the moment you set foot in Sherborne to enquire after Ben. Whoever is behind this may fear you know more than is good for you. He may need to silence you. I need to pay Master Cope a visit. You, Matthias, should go home and collect Elizabeth and Davy and bring them here. You need a place of safety for a few days while we get to the bottom of this. Last night failed – but tomorrow is another day."

"I'm not sure Davy could travel," Matthias said, doubtfully, "Elizabeth was of the opinion that he had broken a rib."

"Nicholas will go with you – and William, if you can wait for him to be a little rested – I hear the hooves in the yard now. Maybe he will have something to add, - and then we need to find the boy before he comes to harm."

Lady Bridget's kitchen was well supplied. Her serving girl produced an acceptable repast of cheese and bread whilst Matthias waited somewhat impatiently for William. He had ridden from Poole, stopping overnight at his sister's house in Wimborne. He was dusty and tired, but quite undismayed on learning that he would have to mount again after a brief rest.

"News, William?" asked Sir Tobias, a frown of concentration knitting his forehead.

"Sketchy only – but useful," William replied, asking with his eyes whether he was free to speak what he had learned in front of Matthias. Sir Tobias gave a slight nod.

"The sea captain is from Poole, and is indeed a true sea captain, plying between Poole and Calais. He carries wool and cloth – and some occasional passengers. He is known to be mostly an honest man, but of late has had money to spend. I spoke with the harbour-master who is a cousin of my sister's husband. He told me that on the last two voyages, the captain, one Ralph of Melcombe – has carried passengers both ways. They seem to be merchants by their dress – they may well be the pair who were overheard at the monastery."

"You saw no-one who resembled Matthias' description of them?"

"No," William replied, "but there is a good deal of trade at Poole, and so many merchants coming and going that it would be hard to pick them out."

"France," said Sir Tobias thoughtfully, "but why Sherborne? We have nothing here worth spying on. The young King rarely comes within miles – his hunting lodge at Gillingham or to visit the Bishop of Salisbury is probably the nearest – and that only with his retinue of protectors and hangers-on."

"Is it to spy or to steal?" Matthias wondered, suddenly.

"If it is to steal, then it must be something worth killing for – or a thing somebody powerful and rich desires and so is prepared to offer good gold for underhand deeds," Sir Tobias declared. He pushed his wine goblet away from him and stood up.

"We linger too long. I must see the Abbot again, - this time more urgently, and I will also call on Master Cope. He will tell me who these customers were, or I shall have him answer to the sheriff. William, Nicholas, - ride with Matthias to bring Davy and Elizabeth here. I would not have deaths where we can prevent them."

It was a hurried party which rode out from Purse Caundle late that morning. Sir Tobias rode with them part of the way, and when they turned into Milborne

Port, he rode on towards Sherborne, anxious to reach the Abbey.

Matthias was relieved beyond belief to find his house still standing, and Davy moving cautiously round the yard, watched by an anxious Elizabeth, but Davy was not at all happy to be asked to ride out to Purse Caundle.

"Suppose this fine house were to be fired in our absence, Master?" he objected, "and I am still very tender. Elizabeth has bound my chest and ribs, but it jars and jolts at every move."

Matthias stood perplexed in his own home. He looked at Davy, pale and sweating from the small amount of exertion of sweeping in the stable yard. He had dark smudges under his eyes and pain lines around his mouth. Even with William and Nicholas to help, he would find the journey of some five miles or so, very painful.

"Sir Tobias was quite definite in his instructions," William stated. He could see and appreciate the indecision in Matthias.

"Somebody has marked you well, Matthias. Would you risk another such attack?"

"I would be more prepared his time," began Matthias.

William's experienced eye ran over him. He saw a young man of determined attitude, strong, fit but untrained in combat.

"Forgive me," he said, "but you were lucky last evening. I think we are talking about hired assassins who have been paid well to do a job. You and Davy fought well, but you were both injured. You do not know whether your attacker sustained any injuries – we must assume not. They – or he – may return tonight to finish what was started yesterday. He will find two assailants who may be ready and waiting, but who are not fully recovered from yesterday, - especially Davy. So you are willing – but weakened. It is unlikely that they will fire the house if they discover it empty – they want you dead to avoid being recognized or discovered. The two men who fired Lydia's home and the two men you overheard in the monastery hostelry were clearly the same. That's twice you could have seen them – they want you gone, Matthias."

Reluctantly, Matthias concurred. He felt but a babe in such things; his well intentioned meddling had led them into danger, and however uncomfortable Davy's journey, it was one he had to make.

Elizabeth damped the fire down and put together a few necessities.

"Only a day or two, I hope," she said, quietly.

William saddled the nag for Davy, and helped Elizabeth up behind himself. As Matthias turned his great house key in the lock, he hoped devoutly that they would return safely very soon.

Chapter 11

Sir Tobias rode straight to Richard Cope's shop. His work as coroner of Dorset was varied and interesting, but he had not encountered a case before which held such genuine intrigue and plotting. He was more accustomed to thefts, and such killings as there were involved jealousies or drunken loutishness. This case was different. He smelled danger and a sinister sense of being watched by unknown persons, for reasons that were as yet unclear to him.

Master Cope greeted him warmly. Sir Tobias was well known for a man who liked the gracious things of life, and who had the wherewithal to afford them. Richard Cope smiled pleasantly, thinking of the fine leather gloves he had at present – ideal for the coroner's lady wife. His smile faded rapidly when he learned the coroner's real business.

"My guild is against allowing people access to our customers," he blustered.

"Nonsense!" Sir Tobias declared, robustly. "The guild is but recently formed – and any guild which helps its members to withhold information needed by the coroner or the sheriff when investigating two murders needs to be disbanded instantly. What have you got to hide, Richard?"

The glover's eyes slid past the coroner and fastened themselves on a distant and indiscriminate piece of sky.

"Why should I hide anything?" he asked.

"That is precisely what I'm asking you!" Sir Tobias snapped.

"Ben was your most experienced apprentice – he was within days of completing his time with you, and you allowed him considerable leeway. He visited customers for you and delivered finished goods. He apparently was absent from the shop longer than need be of recent times. Why?"

"I don't know," Richard Cope replied unhappily. He kept his eyes well away from Sir Tobias.

"Then why did you not reprimand him? You are known to be a good and able master. Why did Ben escape your wrath?"

Master Cope licked his lips nervously. His eyes flickered to a spot on the far side of the street.

"Which was what?" Sir Tobias asked, coldly.

"I cannot explain it to you."

"Oh yes you can," was the swift answer.

"It involves my dealings with Father Samuel and the Abbey church," muttered the glover.

"With Father Samuel and the Abbey..?" echoed Sir Tobias.

"I am in agreement with Father Samuel's objections to the plans for the Abbey relative to All Hallows…"

"How could this lead to murder?" asked Sir Tobias, aghast.

"No, no – I'm sure it did not," Richard Cope said hastily, "Ben discovered my involvement with Father Samuel and my supplying monies for the purchase of the new font erected in All Hallows…..he agreed to say nothing to anyone of any standing if I allowed him to deal with one particular customer."

"And who was this customer?"

"It was nothing – nothing that could offer any solution," Richard Cope said, squirming under Sir Tobias' hard eyes.

"I'm waiting, Master Cope. I don't know who you think you're protecting – Ben is dead. His widow is homeless. The serving girl is dead, and Matthias Barton and his household have been attacked in their own home. The brother of the serving wench is missing – may be even dead as far as I can tell. I need every piece of information I can squeeze out of you. You are scared for your own safety within the town – a town which is becoming divided on a church matter, and your unwillingness to divulge information doesn't become you or this newly formed guild you've become involved with."

Richard Cope flushed deeply. Sir Tobias was a perceptive man – his reluctance was to save his own face within the guild should his small part in Ben's downfall come to light - and to a certain extent – guilt, that allowing Ben access to a customer should have perhaps been instrumental in causing his death. He breathed deeply.

"He wanted to visit the locksmith."

"The locksmith?" Sir Tobias repeated. Enlightenment dawned – could Ben have wanted to have a key made? Was a key the missing part of this whole affair? If they could discover that, they would be halfway to the truth.

"Yes, - he took some fabric samples for him to see, and when he had chosen his style, Ben delivered the finished gloves. They were a gift for his wife."

"When were these visits made?"

"I can't recall," began Richard Cope, beginning to recover his composure, although his hands felt clammy. He was willing the coroner to keep his voice down.

"I think you can" Sir Tobias said, firmly, "Fetch your day book."

"I don't need to," Richard Cope said, giving in wearily, "The samples went out in mid February and the gloves were delivered by Ben just a week before he died. That was the time when he was away for most of the morning."

"Why was it necessary to withhold this information from me?" Sir Tobias demanded. The merchant looked sheepish.

"I resented Master Barton asking me for details of my customers. These newly formed guilds will be powerful tools for the craftsmen and merchants. I didn't want trading information revealed to all and sundry."

"Is there not another reason?" Sir Tobias demanded, sternly. "Did you not think if your plans to support Father Samuel against the Abbot came to light the guild would look badly on you?"

"Oh no – it was not the guild," Master Cope explained, relinquishing any attempt to conceal things from the coroner now, "It was the monks who had befriended Ben. He had formed a friendship with two brothers of which I was aware – and I feared Ben would pass news on to them, thus revealing to the Abbot who had provided the finance for the font and our other plans are by no means complete yet, - nor are we even sure of who is for and who against.. Ben made a promise not to reveal any of this to his new found friends if I allowed him to deal directly with the locksmith."

"What do you think was the importance of the lock-smith to Ben?" Sir Tobias asked, hoping to pump Master Cope further now he had him in a mental stranglehold.

"I presumed he was beginning to try and start a cus-tomer base of his own with one eye on his future , and he knew I wasn't too concerned about retaining Will Shergold. He only has one order each year, - hardly a great loss to me if Ben should want to cultivate him as his first customer."

"Let us return to the friendship with two monks," Sir Tobias pursued, "In your experience as a towns person, is it normal practice for the monks to befriend a humble apprentice?"

Master Cope looked surprised, as if he had not con-sidered it before.

Well, - no." he admitted, a little dejected that he hadn't thought of that point himself.

"Can you describe these two monks to me?" asked the coroner., but Master Cope was unable to offer any more information at all – a cowled monk in a town with a large abbey was very like any other cowled monk, and he had never seen either of them at close quarters. It was obvious to Sir Tobias that Ben had thought them to be genuine brothers from the Abbey, - whether they were or not he hoped soon to be able to tell.

With Richard Cope now able to look him in the eye, Sir Tobias felt he could gain no more information from the glover..

Will Shergold was the next port of call, and Will was easy meat. He had nothing to hide, and he was secretly rather frightened by the sight of the coroner at his shop door. He had also liked Ben and been both surprised and saddened by his death.

"Ben needed a key copied and cut," he told Sir Tobias, with no attempt at subterfuge.

"He asked me to do it in February, but it was only a week before he died that he actually brought the key in. He waited while I did it. He said it had to be returned the same day."

"Did he seem nervous while he was waiting?" the coroner asked.

"Oh no," Will answered, "he was in a happy mood. He sat here and drank some ale and we chatted."

"What did you chat about?"

"Nothing of any importance," said Will, frowning hard to remember.

"Think, Will," pleaded Sir Tobias, "The key may hold the answer. Have you any idea where the original came from?"

"I believe it came from the Abbey," said Will, with some hesitation. It was his first moment of hesitation, so he added, "I cannot be sure, - Ben was evasive, but I had a feeling that he had some business with the Abbey. I saw him meet with one of the brothers immediately after he'd taken the key... they stopped on the corner opposite the shop and talked for several minutes."

"He didn't pass the key over to the monk?"

"Oh, no. I saw nothing pass between them. Ben had a bag containing glove samples, and he had slipped the key into this.'

Sir Tobias smiled, and had to be content with that. There was no guile in Will Shergold, and he had obtained all the information he needed.

His last visit was to Abbot Bradford. He was not well received. Abbot Bradford was preparing for Easter mass, parish baptisms, which were a very lucrative source of income for the Abbey, and Easter processionals. He was determined not to give an inch to the Bishop's instructions that the doorway should be widened until they were ready to obey the order to remove the new font which had been placed in Allhallows. He hoped his Easter sermons would leave them in no doubt as to who was in charge. It seemed that they were at an impasse.

He was even less welcoming when he learned that Sir Tobias had come

"I can promise you that all my monks are honest, and quite above consorting with mere apprentices of the town," he said, stiffly.

Sir Tobias tried another avenue.

"Abbot Bradford, - what secrets do you hold from the King's advisors?"

"None, my dear Sir Tobias. Sherborne is a very backwater compared with other Southern towns. That I can certainly vouch for. We have not had the pleasure of a visit from any representative of the young King for many, many months – running into years."

Sir Tobias thought carefully.

"Then what do you hold in the Abbey that is of value?"

"Priceless vestments...silver plate.." replied Abbot Bradford, proudly, "all carefully counted and locked away from prying eyes when necessary."

"Nothing more? No gold... precious stones... relics?"

The Abbot shook his head.

"We are not so rich as some abbeys and monasteries within riding distance of here," he said. "If thieves were to break in to our coffers, they would be disappointed with their haul. We have nothing else of value here."

Sir Tobias had to be content with that.

Much later, a dark robed figure slipped silently from the nave of the Abbey and into the monastery by an unlocked side door – one he had unlocked himself earlier in the day. The cloisters were silent and deserted for the moment, it being between offices. No-one saw him. The monks were mostly at private prayer or uneasy sleep, and he had deliberately chosen an evening during Holy Week, knowing that even these pampered brothers would be more devout during this time.

The door he needed was locked. He stood still outside the heavy oak door, feeling the cold hinges... pressing his face into the fragrant wood. He slipped his hand into the deep pocket of his robe, and closed it on the key. It was his, and his alone. He breathed the cold, crisp air. It filled his lungs cleanly as he paused for a moment's delicious anticipation. The sky seen through the cloister arches was deeply , darkly blue, the stars splintering brightly through the velvet night. This would be a sweet moment.

He slipped the key carefully into the lock and turned it slowly and carefully to avoid making noise. He stepped into the unlocked room, and swung the door noiselessly shut behind him.

The boy Roger turned uneasily on the cold, damp flagstones. His back was sore and bleeding where he had been beaten. His ankles were bound to prevent his escape. The tiny room was dark and silent. The rough ropes chafed his ankles so that any movement was excrutiatingly painful.

His belly ached from hunger; his eyes were sore from crying, but crying was no use to him. He had no idea where he was, but he knew what they wanted – they wanted the key that he had promised to steal for them. How easy it had seemed three months ago , - a little key was all they wanted, - and they'd promised a handsome sum of gold for it. His problem had been that he didn't know where it was kept. Then two monks had sought him out unexpectedly and had told him where to find it, and in his cleverness, he'd managed to steal it from under the Abbot's very nose – or rather, belt. It had all fallen so neatly into place, or so it had seemed to Roger, the clever boy-thief. Mary had arranged that Ben Glover would copy the key immediately Roger obtained it, and Roger had re-placed the original with no great difficulty. He'd been lucky to find Ben – it was Mary who suggested asking Ben to help, although Mary didn't have the faintest idea that she was helping to copy a stolen key. Mary just knew Ben could arrange to copy a key through his work, and might be interested in earning a little extra money.

But it hadn't turned out like that. The two monks had insisted on seeing Ben and asking him to do extra things for them... like find other information about the movements of the brothers during evening hours. That was when Roger had begun to feel a little afraid, and had realised that these two monks were not all they seemed, but he hadn't confided his fear to anyone, - the pull of the promised gold was too great.

Ben had found that new task very tedious, - he wasn't privy to the movement in the Abbey, and in addition to that, Ben was supposed to have handed the copied key over, and he hadn't done that for some reason – and now Ben was dead. Mary should have known where Ben had concealed the key, - but even Mary was dead now. As long as Roger could convince the men that he did know where the key was and could lead them to it, he was sure he would live, but the beatings were getting more and more savage each time they came. He wasn't sure how long he'd been here, - it was too dark to count the days and nights, but it seemed a long time. He moved uncomfortably again, aware that he was lying in his own excrement. When would the monks return?

Chapter 12

Davy tossed uneasily in the little back room where he and Elizabeth were housed, together with Sir Tobias' serving man.

His ribs pained him; it was difficult to breathe without pain, and images of Ben, blind drunk in front of the abbey, kept flashing through his mind. There were no drapes at the windows of the room, and branches scraped across the outer fabric of the building, setting his jangled nerves on fire.

What had Ben said to him in between bouts of drunken retching? Davy wished he could remember, - wished he'd paid more attention.....and suppose Master Barton's fine house was fired whilst they were away? He shouldn't have agreed to leave, -.....it was folly...first Ben, then Lydia...Mary...the attack... images swam in Davy's hot and tired eyes. His brain wandered back and forth, teasing hidden information. Elizabeth lay still beside him, aware that he was awake, but reluctant to speak. She was shaken and disturbed herself – no words could help Davy's pain. Let him lie, and drift asleep.

And so, eventually, he did – into a troubled, aching void.

Ben was chasing him past the abbey which was a towering inferno of flames. A monk on horseback rode after them, dragging kegs of beer. Lydia had grown huge

– seven foot tall at least, - and she appeared from nowhere, throwing gold coins at him. Elizabeth had disappeared into the burning abbey, and Davy had to reach her before the flames swallowed her.

He woke as the early light filtered into the room, soaked with sweat, his head pounding as hard as his heart. Elizabeth had already risen and was striving to make herself useful in Sir Tobias' household.

Davy lay still, knowledge of where he was gradually flooding his consciousness. Ben had been shouting slurred words, - something to do with a book. It made no sense to Davy at all. What did Ben want with a book? He couldn't read.

Davy swung his legs cautiously over the side of the bed and bracing himself on the stones of the wall, stood up. Great God! But he didn't know how many muscles you used just to stand up! Pulling his rough night shirt up cost him some stabbing aches, - luckily Elizabeth had had the forethought to leave a piss pot by the bed. At least relieving himself gave him pleasure – he didn't have to move.

Dressing in his simple tunic and hose caused some unpleasant twinges, but at last he was able to unlatch the door and venture into the large kitchen.

Elizabeth was watching for him – she had heard his faltering sounds of movement, and she indicated a place for him to sit at the big scrubbed table around which five or six servants sat, with mugs of watered ale and coarse bread. William was with them, but in a chair apart from the table, and Davy noticed he had some slices of cheese with his bread.

After breaking his fast with Sir Tobias' servants, Davy moved closer to William. The older man looked tired – Davy felt sorry that he should have had to make another journey for him, after returning from the coast.

"Are you rested, Davy?" William asked, kindly.

"Not much, but I'll do," Davy replied, drawing a cautious breath.

"William, I need some counsel over a matter concerning my friend Ben."

William stood up.

"Walk outside with me, Davy."

The two men slipped out of the kitchen and into the cobbled courtyard, Davy wondering how he was ever going to walk again without clutching hold of door posts and corners of walls. There was a pump in the courtyard, and Davy marked it in his mind as a suitable place for a wash in due course, when he could bend over without wincing.

"I work for Sir Tobias," William warned him, "whatever you tell me cannot be kept from him."

"I understand that, but just counsel my conscience,"

William nodded, and waited.

"I had need of searching for Ben one afternoon, about a month ago. He had not returned home, and Lydia was afraid. It was a Saturday,and he should have been home from Sherborne early in the morning. I walked into Sherborne – it was becoming wet and cold by then, - and eventually I found Ben on the green in front of the Abbbey. He was shouting and hollering rubbish – blind drunk he was. Ben wasn't given to excessive drinking – I tried to lead him away but he shrugged me off – he didn't recognize me – and then he puked up all over the grass, - over and over and over."

Davy paused for breath, remembering the sour smell of vomit on the rain-wet green.

"When he'd finished, he wiped his mouth and asked me why they expected him to carry the damned book. He was talking nonsense – I fetched some water and stripped his shirt off – it was befouled with vomit – and bathed his head and mouth. After a bit he was easier, and he seemed to know me. We sheltered under the abbey walls out of the wind."

"What then?" William asked, as Davy seemed lost in the remembering.

"Ben slept on my shoulder for an hour or so – and then woke with a blinding head-ache. He made me swear to say nothing of the incident to anyone – I thought he was ashamed of it – so I promised. It was bitterly cold as it grew dark, and Ben just needed to sleep, so I helped him to his lodging and put him in his bed. Luckily we didn't see Mistress Fosse, his lodging lady, for I slept on the floor beside him for very fear of making the walk back to Milborne Port in the dark. Next morning we woke early and crept out of the house, and returned to Milborne Port. Lydia and Elizabeth were so relieved to see us that they assumed we had just had too much ale, but Ben made me swear over and over that I'd tell no-one of the incident. I've kept that promise. William, Ben is dead. Do you think this might be of some importance?"

William was silent for a short while.

"I don't know, Davy. It may throw some light on it – the ale was certainly doing the talking, but Sir Tobias is privy to a great many matters that concern the war, the young King, the Abbot and this area generally. Let him be the judge – and your own young master is no fool. The two of them together may piece the matter into some shape."

Davy was silenced by his grave words.

"Do you really think this could be King's business?" he asked, "here, in Sherborne? We are small and insignificant, and tucked away…"

"King's business is everywhere, Davy," William replied, "but like you, I would doubt it. But let Sir Tobias be the judge of that. He is mindful of such matters."

The two men went inside, and William went through into the main house to seek out Sir Tobias.

He found them deep in conversation by the fire, Sir Tobias noting items of importance on his fingers. He looked up as William entered.

"Ah, William, - I've just spent time with Matthias going over events…"

"A little piece of information from Davy might fit into the puzzle," interrupted William, although there was doubt in his voice. Matthias looked up, startled.

"From Davy?" he asked, in surprise.

"He'll tell you himself, - it's best," William said, and on a nod from Sir Tobias he returned to the kitchen to fetch Davy.

"Now don't be put out, Matthias," warned Sir Tobias, a friendly arm touching Matthias, "You'll find he thought it was nothing – and William obviously thinks otherwise."

Davy was ill at ease and somewhat sheepish, having to re-tell the events as he related them to William. He glanced several times at Matthias as if to satisfy himself that his master was not about to explode with anger, but Matthias, forewarned by Sir Tobias, sat slumped in his chair, chin on hands, listening intently to Davy's account. He even managed to bite his tongue at the end, when he really wanted to ask Davy why he hadn't mentioned this before.

Sir Tobias said nothing when Davy had finished. His legs were astride his chair, his head tilted back, his arms folded across his chest.

"Let's re-construct." He announced, looking at his ceiling.

"Imagine. Ben is a trusted employee – an apprentice nearing the end of his time and looking to catch customers of his own. His work is satisfactory. His life is in order. His wife is with child. Some-one puts a simple idea to him that will make a little extra money. Ben is tempted. Let's say it's Mary's brother Roger – the clever little thief. Maybe Roger is asked by some-one – whom we do not know yet, - to steal what in this case appears to be a key. He has no access to this key. Why? But he knows someone who has – Ben – and he can reach Ben through his own sister Mary, who is the serving girl in the house where Ben lodges."

He paused.

"Why would Ben have access?" Matthias queried, frowning.

"Because he is being given greater access to customers now he is reaching the end of his apprenticeship , and he lodges and works in Sherborne. Maybe the observer knows that Ben could have an easy in-out to wherever the key is for. The key has something to do with the abbey – and Ben had a duplicate made of this key."

"Did Ben have access to a customer at the abbey?" William asked.

"Apparently not, but they may have realised that he could make a reason to go into the Abbey," Sir Tobias said, "but I can twist Richard Cope's arm no further. He told me about the locksmith. I really think now that he knows no more that can be of value to us."

The little party were silent for a few moments, pondering Sir Tobias' assessment of the situation. Sir Tobias continued, "Ben obtained, we presume, the key. He had it copied as instructed and returned the original without being detected – or so we assume. He must have told Mary that he had the key so that she could pass the information on to his overlords, whoever they are."

So far the story seemed simple – but why had it led to murder? And not just one murder, but two, an attempted murder by burning and the disappearance of Roger.

"It becomes more sinister now," said Matthias. He felt uneasy here – he had a home of his own – his father's inheritance for him. Was it safe to have left it?

"Indeed it does," agreed Sir Tobias. "It appears to be more than a village squabble over a filched key. Ben was murdered . Why? Was he perhaps waiting for more instructions, but *saw* who was behind this intrigue? Did he guess at more than he was supposed to, and threaten to call in the sheriff? Or did he perhaps try to double cross his overlord, thinking his trouble was worth more money? Was that why he was murdered? And murder implies a dangerous mission . King's business? I doubt it. Your father was once involved in King's business, Matthias – it tailed off some years before he died. Oh No," he hastened, before Matthias could even raise the question, "I did not know him. I know *of* him from certain enquiries I have had to make recently."

He forbore to say what these were, and Matthias wisely did not ask.

"The young king has protectors, as you know, and only comes into his own this year. Gloucester will argue and bicker over the protectorate for some months to come. I only hope young Henry will emerge a strong and just king, but only time will tell."

Privately Sir Tobias had serious doubts and many fears, but to air them would be treason, even in this select gathering. There were many tales of disaster and defeat in the closing wars with France, and numerous small lawless bands of deserting soldiers appearing near sea ports. William had brought such tales back from Poole, but now was not the time to discuss these.

"So if not King's business, then what else?" Matthias wondered.

"Bishop's business. War spoils. French spy business," William surmised.

Sir Tobias nodded. "The abbey plays a significant part in this matter – we may be sure of that. I believe trade,- or illicit trade – with France probably makes up the other part of the story."

"The only kind of trade there is with France at present is illicit," muttered William, darkly.

"I must visit the good Abbot yet again," Sir Tobias said, with a wry smile. "The key holds the secret, and Ben's mutterings do begin to make some sense to me, but first I must visit Abbot Bradford and make sure of some facts."

He rose from his seat and straightened his clothing about him.

"William, ride with me. Davy, stay here and rest your bruised ribs, - and Matthias, enjoy some quiet reading until I return. You two have been somewhat battered, and you are unaccustomed to this strange life of action!"

After William and Sir Tobias had ridden off, Matthias felt unsettled and restless. Davy had returned to the servant's hall, and he was left alone. He became much more certain that his own home was at risk, and he determined to ride over to Milborne Port in Sir Tobias' absence to put his mind at rest, and maybe to do a little work while he was there.

He took the journey steadily, lost in his own thoughts. There were travellers on the road heading towards Sherborne, for it was nearly Easter, and Mass would be much celebrated over the period. The guesten hall would surely be full, and maybe the newly formed guilds would dare to stand up to Abbot Bradford and oppose his narrowing of the doorway., or maybe the new font would be used.

The gateway to Barton Holding swung open. Matthias frowned. He thought they'd locked it very carefully. A chill caution overcame him as he swung down from the saddle. His newly glassed window by the great front door was smashed, and as he entered, the breeze blew in, rustling papers and books lying around. The room had been ransacked, - boxes of his father's papers were lying in confusion, rustled by the air from the window which had provided entry for the intruder. He stood still, listening in the silence, but he heard no sound, felt no breath of an intruder. Who-ever had been there had left. Matthias knew the search had been for the key, - but how had the search led here, to his house? Sir Tobias had been right – he was being watched – he had been followed.

He went from room to room, and the picture was the same in each room – disturbed chests, bedding flung aside, pictures moved – the search had been thorough. All Matthias' careful preparations for his young scholars was destroyed. The cupboard where the horn books and inks were stored was smashed, and the contents spilled and broken. His matting had been disrupted as if whoever had searched had believed a key could be hidden under the flooring. The kitchen rushes were pushed to one side, and in one place, even the earthen floor had been well prodded. The search had been devastatingly thorough.

Grimly, Matthias found the cloth he had chosen so carefully in the market and stuffed it firmly into the hole in the window. Glass was still expensive, and he'd been very proud of his glassed windows. They let in more light than parchment, and he'd needed the maximum light for his scholars. That done, he locked the door firmly behind him and re-mounted his horse. He would return tomorrow with Davy and Elizabeth. Any danger they may have been in had surely passed. The thief had found nothing.

Chapter 13

Abbot Bradford was most displeased at yet another visit from the Coroner.

"Sir Tobias, I beg of you.." he began, stiffly, "I am preparing for the Easter Mass."

"..And I am preparing to catch a murderer," Sir Tobias retorted.

Abbot Bradford sat, finger tips together, eyes half closed to imply that if he must suffer, he would do so very obviously

"Very well," with an ill concealed sigh, "What is it you require this time?"

"Tell me of the visit made to the Abbey by Ben Glover. Whom did he see? What did he deliver?"

Abbot Bradford opened his yes in genuine amazement.

"I have no idea," he said, and his surprise was not feigned.

"I did not know the young man – if he delivered something here, it was certainly not to any of the brothers."

Sir Tobias tried again.

"So. What do you have in the Abbey which might be *really* worth stealing? Not petty baubles, - but something precious enough to kill for."

The Abbot bridled at his words.

"You speak of "petty baubles" – there are no petty baubles connected with the work of God."

"Oh, come, Abbot Bradford," sighed Sir Tobias, "Let's not argue. You know what I mean – I don't mean altar cloths, silver vestments, candlesticks. There must be something of real value here."

"There are many beautiful things in the House of God," said the Abbot, piously, "The

"Do you keep or possess coffers of silver or gold?" Sir Tobias asked, becoming puzzled.

"Such things are long gone," the Abbot replied.

"The rents and tithings from your holdings are worth much money," hazarded Sir Tobias. Abbot Bradford inclined his head.

"The rents and tithings are dealt with by the bailiff and are not kept here in the Abbey".

"Is your bailiff honest?"

Again, Abbot Bradford made every appearance of being affronted at the suggestion.

"What do you have here that would need help to carry away? Sir Tobias asked. He had Ben's drunken gabblings in the back of his mind, although he had largely dismissed them as being of no great account.

Abbot Bradford allowed himself the ghost of a smile. It did not soften his face and no warmth appeared in his eyes. "The altar itself, I suppose, some of the great candlesticks, our missal…"

Sir Tobias held up a hand.

"Wait!" he said, "Your missal! A BOOK!"

Abbot Bradford managed to look sorrowful.

"More than a mere book, Sir Tobias." Our missal is a work of art. You have not seen it? It is indeed a thing of beauty. It was completed by two monks 30 years ago, and is a fine piece of copying and illustration. John

Whas was one of our own monks and the other –
Sifrewas – a most imaginative man."

He spoke reverently.

"Each page is indeed a work of perfection, - but the
missal is in daily use and the book itself weighs nearly
three stone – too heavy to steal and ride away with in
your hand."

"May I see this book?" Sir Tobias asked.

The Abbot sighed in exasperation.

"We keep it locked in one of our chambers , and the
monks move it on special celebration days"

"May I see the book?" Sir Tobias repeated.

The Abbot rose.

"Follow me," he said, with ill-concealed irritation.

Sir Tobias followed the Abbot to a small door set in a
stone wall leading from one of the side chapels. He
selected a key from his belt and inserted it into the lock.
The door opened easily.

The room contained a wooden table upon which lay
a great book, open at the offices of the day. Sir Tobias
could see the vivid illuminations on the page, overlaid
with gold leaf and lovingly and imaginatively illustrated
with leaves, birds and fruits. The luminosity of the page
gleamed with glory and worship. This was truly the
work of the Almighty – a great and awesome tribute to
the magnificence of the power of prayer.

The Coroner was silent as he took in the sheer beauty
of the book.

"This missal is used from time to time, Abbot?" he
enquired.

"Yes, indeed," was the cold reply.

"Did you never consider it a thing of such worth that
it might be stolen?"

Abbot Bradford fell silent.

"To be frank, no, Sir Tobias, I hadn't. It is a remarkable and beautiful book – we are very fortunate to possess such a thing, - but it is kept here and carried out in procession by the brothers, and then returned here and locked in after use. No, - I do not think this is a thing which could be stolen."

Sir Tobias met his eyes. Despite the Abbot's aloofness, they were honest eyes.

"I believe you may be wrong," Sir Tobias said, flatly.

The Abbot raised his eyebrows. Sir Tobias laid a hand reverently on the great book.

"Young Ben was killed for a key," he said. "I think it may have been the key to this room."

"Impossible!" the Abbot declared. "There is only one key and it remains on my belt, which is never away from me."

"And at night?" asked Sir Tobias.

"It is in my room," conceded the Abbot, "But no-one enters my room at night."

"..as far as you are aware.." commented Sir Tobias.

"I do not think it would be possible," the Abbot said, austerely,

"Does no lay person enter your room when you are sleeping?" Sir Tobias persisted.

"Not one!" the Abbot declared.

Sir Tobias tore his eyes away from the magnificence on the page, and allowed the Abbot to lock the do"Please be very vigilant concerning strangers," he told the Abbot, as he took his leave.

Roger opened his eyes with difficulty. The last beating he'd had caused one eye to close up, and it was sticky with blood, pus and sweat. He moved uneasily in the darkened room, and groaned in pain. Dimly he made out the shape of an unglassed window through which he could see one or two stars. Every attempt to move shot bolts of pain through him, and it was several minutes before he realised that he was bound with coarse hemp to a narrow truckle, making the window impossible to reach. The knots cut into the flesh of his wrists and ankles. One side of his left hip was sore beyond imagining, caused when he'd tried to run and his captors had felled him cruelly and dragged him across a patch of rough gravel.

He was mentally and physically exhausted; he could scarcely remember why he was here, let alone where he was.

He had fouled his own garments with excrement again, and moving his body was unpleasant beyond belief. His belly ached for food – his throat was parched with thirst. Worse still, he now knew beyond a shadow of doubt who was the prime mover behind his captivity. This was no longer a game – this was deadly to the death.

Roger's resistance was at its lowest ebb; the stench of the darkened cell was unbearable – if it was a cell, - he couldn't really be so sure – and the silence around him was suffocating. He had no sense of the passage of time, intermittently falling into a semi-conscious state.

Some time late in the night the door swung open stealthily, and a hooded figure gazed dispassionately at the swollen lips, bruised eyes and feverish breathing.

"Little fool," a voice hissed, venomously, "Did you think you could double-cross me? You and the apprentice. - this is no market place game. I have endured this English way of life for two years for this prize."

The knife was swift; it found its mark.

The door closed again, leaving the dying boy alone in the dark.

Matthew left Sir Tobias' home the next day without Davy, who was to stay another day or two to complete his recovery, Elizabeth remaining with him. They had been made most welcome by the serving household, and Elizabeth was learning new skills in Lady Bridget's kitchen.

William travelled with him, and the two men regarded Matthias' ransacked home with weary resignation.

"Whoever is behind this is very desperate for the key," William said, as they began the task of setting furniture to rights and clearing broken glass, locks and spilled contents.

"I must have been marked out as a possible recipient on the night they fired Lydia's house," Matthew mused. "How else could I have been connected to Ben?"

He pondered this after William had left.

Who could have connected him with Ben?

He ticked off the likely contacts in his mind.

Thomas Copeland? Impossible. He'd been in his house to ask questions, so Thomas knew he had an interest in Ben's death.

Richard Cope? Possible, - but what motive? Richard Cope was a respected merchant with no need for dishonest dealings, and Sir Tobias clearly felt him to be beyond murder. His reluctance to talk was probably no more than a wariness of too many people knowing his trading capabilities. After all, there were several glove-makers in the town.

Abbot Bradford? Out of the question – although certainly the Abbot was resentful of the questionings made by Sir Tobias and himself. He was aware that Abbot Bradford was not party to him being involved in the investigation, but that was insufficient for him to persuade anyone to meddle in Matthias' affairs.

Could Mistress Fosse possibly be involved in some way? Matthias thought not, although Roger had been there, and she may have mentioned Matthias and Davy to him.

Mary certainly was involved, and young Roger, who still had not turned up, - but Mary had died for her involvement before Matthias had become entangled in this strange mesh.

Mary's family? Hardly likely, given Davy's account of his visit there, and the presence of the young priest supporting the family.

Who else had Matthias spoken to, or been seen by? There were the two men who had fired Lydia's house, although it had been dark, and recognition afterwards would not have been easy.

Had he been recognized or pointed out by some-one at Lydia's funeral? Or when he'd visited the guesten hall? He seemed to have met a blank wall. Some-one had connected him with the missing key – someone had seen him with Davy or with Sir Tobias. Some-one had been watching him. Someone he knew and had not thought of suspecting.....no answers came to him, and he slept uneasily that night.

The missal's pages were turned quietly in the pale moonlight that shone into the room where it lay. The hands which caressed each vellum sheet were gentle and reverent. The eyes which devoured the richly decorated pages were moist with awe, overwhelmed by the perfection on each page. Birds, their colours and shapes, all so perfect; angels, devils, saints, knights, all depicted in meticulous detail...fruits flowers and leaves, entwined round the carefully scripted letters, each one illuminated in rich golds, reds and blues.....here a little cameo of Abbot Brunyng kneeling in prayer, in the margin there was another of the good bishop of Salisbury....such perfection. There was the infant Christchild with the blessed virgin...and later, the crucified Christ, . All this and so much more, throat-catching in its vivid beauty and glory. How could one leave sch perfection behind? He turned another page carefully...there....Saint Wulsin.... St. Silvester....St. Benedict....colours sumptuous and costly, assailed him from the pages. Intricate illustrations of gospel scenes spoke to him with such clarity.

After a quiet prayer, the reader sighed with the disappointment of having to leave such perfection behind.

The door was carefully locked with Mary's key.

Davy and Elizabeth were welcomed home by Matthias the next day. Davy was considerably better, and Elizabeth was delighted to be home, setting out at once to clean up and re-instate furnishings wherever she could.

Sir Tobias sent word with Davy that he had visited Master Cope a second time and had found him evasive, but on a third visit, the house was locked and there was no sign of life there – suspicious. Did Richard Cope know more than he had told them – or was he simply afraid that his employment of Ben had put him in mortal danger? There had been no sightings of the boy, Roger. The trail had gone cold.

The next day being Good Friday, Matthias determined to ride down into Sherborne to Mass. He was curious to see how the townspeople's arguments with Abbot Bradford would end, and he was anxious to shake off the lethargic mood which had overtaken him since he had returned home to discover all his work for the forthcoming pupils destroyed.

The Abbey was full, but there would be no processional from Allhallows until Sunday, when there would be baptisms. Matthias slipped inside and stood near a pillar to observe the townspeople, and to hear Mass himself.

He arrived just as the monks filed in procession from the monastery into the Great Abbey. He leaned against the cool pillar and tried to focus his mind on Christ's passion. He was tired, and the monk's chanting mesmerized him into a state of semi-consciousness. They were passing him now...the plain song was beautiful.. regular..full of dignified pathos...

Matthias found himself counting the pairs of monks as they passed him, processing down to the choir.... ...seven...eight...nine...ten...eleven...twelve...thirteen....they were past him, their robes swinging gently in time to their rehearsed, measured walk.

His mind woke with a jolt. Thirteen? There should only have been twelve of them....Sir Tobias had mentioned a complement of twenty four monks, yet twenty six had processed.

He eased himself away from the pillar and glanced round at the people nearest to him. Did he know anyone? No, just ordinary townsmen and their wives and families, standing in the knave....no-one was watching him. He slipped surreptitiously out of the door. His horse was tethered nearby. Matthias mounted, and was about to dig his heels into his horse's flanks when he noticed Thomas Copeland advancing across the green towards him. He waved his hands at Matthias from a distance to attract his attention and to prevent him from moving off.

Matthias waited, wondering why Thomas was not at Mass himself.

"Matthias – Oh, I'm so glad to see you! I need the Coroner's help I fear, - can you fetch him?"

"I'm on my way to see him now," Matthias said, "What is the matter, Thomas?"

"I'm afraid it is very urgent, Matthias. Two of my boys have an unpleasant tale to tell which may throw some light on Roger's wherabouts."

"May I hear their story before I go to Purse Caundle?" Matthias asked.

He walked up Cheap Street with Thomas. A little way from Thomas' house, he wrinkled his nose in disgust.

"Have some of your neighbours a passion for long dead fish during Lent?" he asked. The smell was so strong that he pressed his nose into the sleeve of his gown.

In contrast, the inside of Thomas' house was cool and fragrant, - Hannah was a good housekeeper, and she made sure the rushes were changed, herbs strewn among them and all linens were clean and fresh.

Thomas took Matthias into the schoolroom where two boys were sitting, copying laboriously from a slate.

"Masters Goram and Slater are detained as punishment," Thomas told Matthias, "They took their beating well, for I will not tolerate truancy. However, during their truancy, they heard things which you may wish to ask your friend the Coroner to act upon."

Matthias breathed a little faster. Was this the breakthrough they had been waiting for?

"Master Goram, tell Master Barton how you left my house."

The boy looked up from his work.

"We climbed out of Slater's window," he said sullenly. "It was a dare from some-one."

"Go on," Matthias said, eying him severely, for the boy's tone was anything but obedient and penitent.

"The roof was too steep, so we skirted the next house by the overhang, and came down two doors away."

Matthias and Thomas waited.

"At the back of that house, there was a terrible moaning and crying sound and we had to pause in case we were heard, - but there was no window. Then as we slithered down, it sounded as if someone was being thrashed – much harder then Master Copeland thrashes us."

He glanced up slyly as he said this, hoping to curry favour from his schoolmaster, but Thomas' face was impassive.

"When was this?" Matthias asked.

"Two days ago," the boy replied.

Matthias' eyes widened in surprise.

"And you've only just mentioned it?"

Master Goram had the grace to look a little penitent.

"It didn't seem important," he muttered. "We were disciplined, and that's all that matters."

"Part of their discipline was to call on the owners of the next two houses to ascertain whether their escapade had caused any damage," Thomas explained. "I know my immediate neighbour well, but the next house changes occupants quite regularly. When they called, the house was shuttered and empty."

Matthias digested this piece of information in silence.

"Have you searched the garden for any sign of disturbance?" he asked.

Thomas shook his head.

"No, but when I heard about the missing lad, I wondered whether he could have found his way in there to hide."

Matthias stood up.

"Can you arrange for a messenger to be sent to Purse Caundle, to fetch Sir Tobias?" he asked Thomas.

"I'll risk my reputation and break in to take a look for the missing boy, but I'd be far happier if Sir Tobias was on the way in case I am accused of trespass."

Thomas arranged for a messenger to depart immediately, and the two men then skirted the garden of the house in Cheap Street. It was not so neat or kempt as Thomas' own. Although the garden was overgrown, Matthias observed no sign of a scuffle or beating down of greenery. If this was where Roger was being held, he had entered by the front door. Matthias pressed his nose to his sleeve again.

"This dreadful odour is coming from here," he said, as they knocked on the front door.

"I hope to God that doesn't mean a plague house," Thomas murmured, swallowing hard, and burying his nose in his hands.

There was, predictably, no answer, and no sound of movement from within.

There was a foothold at the back, and Matthias hauled himself up to a small window. It was glassed, and the room within appeared to be empty. Balling his fist, and using his cloak to protect his knuckles, Matthias broke the window. The odour became a stench.... Matthias finally recognized it as the stench of death.

"There is something very wrong here, Thomas," he said, "but where is it coming from?"

They stood still, listening. There was no sound but the sound of silence, which seemed to roar in their ears like thunder.

Matthias looked around the dimly lit ground floor. It was an open hall, much the same as many houses would have, and no efforts had been made to hang tapestries or wallhangings to divide the space into individual rooms; the fireplace was cold but on the floor in two neat piles were clothes of the type merchants wore. Matthias recognized them and thought immediately of the two extra monks he had seen in the procession.

There was a stair leading to an upper floor, and Thomas crossed the floor and mounted the wooden steps, Matthias close behind him.

A room at the top of the stairway would obviously have been, in better times, a family solar. Now, it was empty and damp, devoid of any life or warmth. To the left of the stairwell a narrow passage ran, along which was a second doorway – once presumably a small guest or child's room. The door was locked, but the two men guessed that this room would yield up the source of the gut-wrenching smell.

CHAPTER 13

They tried their shoulders against the door, but it would not budge. The wood was not in perfect condition, but the lock held fast.

"Halloo!" Thomas called, "Is there any one there? Can you answer me?"

There was no reply.

"I have a terrible misgiving," Matthias said, "that this may be the missing brother of Mary. My second misgiving is that we have found him too late."

He took his dagger to the wood, and that, teamed with the constant battering they gave the door, yielded a split in the wood, which they were able to enlarge sufficiently to enable them to see into the room.

It was a dark room with no windows. Where there had once been a window were crude wooden boards. A filthy truckle was visible on the far side of the room, and they had no need of candle-light to see that it was blood-soaked. Roger lay as if asleep, his throat cut with a neatness and competence that Matthias found chilling. Rats had been gnawing at his extremities, and even as they peered through the hole they had made, two rats glared at them with red eyes and scuttled away. The stench of death, excrement and stale air made both men retch heavily, and they backed down the stairway, hands clapped over their mouths.

Matthias leaned on the wall outside in the shabby little garden, fighting the urge to vomit. He was sweating with revulsion and fear, but anger soon took over, - anger at himself for being so amateurish and selfish in his search for Roger.

Thomas Cope, an older and gentler personality altogether, retired to the overgrown bushes at one side of the garden and came back several minutes later, wiping his mouth on a handful of fresh grass.

"We'll stay here and await Sir Tobias," Matthias decided. They spoke little as they waited. Sounds from the street and from the distant abbey reached them in a muted way. Leaving the front door open released some of the fetid smell of the house. Matthias' mind dwelt on his own ineptitude and lack of purpose...he could have done....should have done more to find Roger and prevent this tragedy. Thomas sat weakly on the stone wall by the side of the house, eyes closed. He was unused to such violence.

Shortly after noon, Sir Tobias arrived with the Abbot's bailiff, and William.

The bailiff looked shaken.

"This house was purchased by the Abbey a year ago," he told them.

"It is to be repaired and let in the fullness of time. I had no idea there was anyone using it."

Sir Tobias and William mounted the stairs, with Matthias behind them. His mind-set was firmly against vomiting. Thomas stayed outside, anxious now for his young scholars.

Sir Tobias nodded to the Abbot's bailiff, who produced a key and unlocked the partially smashed door. The men looked down on Roger – such a clever thief. Whoever was behind all this had certainly not allowed Roger to get in his way.

Sir Tobias bent close to the boy. Matthias was both amazed and impressed that he could do so – the smell and sight of the lad was never the prettiest thing.

"I believe he was asleep – or unconscious when his throat was slit," he said. "There is no sign of a struggle to defend himself. Look at his face, - he was beaten savagely."

Roger's blackened features were strangely out of focus to Matthias, but he swallowed hard and tried to concentrate.

"He had been beaten all over with a buckled strap, I should think", William said, stepping forward.

"The Abbey knew nothing of this," the bailiff blustered.

"The Abbot must tell me so himself," said Sir Tobias.

The bailiff swallowed nervously. Sir Tobias straightened up.

"Send for two tithing men," he ordered. "The cadaver must be removed, and the house sealed up for further investigation."

As Matthias followed Sir Tobias down the stairs, he couldn't help but think how glad he was that the old laws of first finder were no longer held.

Thomas was pleased to be able to scurry back to his own house after first giving Sir Tobias an account of his boys' story. Sir Tobias would see the boys for himself later, and hear their story first-hand, he told Thomas.

The tithing men arrived, and Sir Tobias watched them with an eagle eye as they gingerly removed Roger's mutilated and bruised body from the stinking room. On Sir Tobias' direction, the body was taken to the town death house. Although he still feared Abbey involvement, the Abbey had no reason to wash and house the body of a boy from Oborne.

Matthias, somewhat recovered after his distressing discovery, told Sir Tobias of his counting of the monks. They were mounted and ready to journey home.

Sir Tobias stared at Matthias as he spoke.

"We're closing in, Matthias. I really believe we're closing in. Someone is after a great treasure in the Abbey. I believe it to be the missal. Ben spoke of a book, didn't he? The missal is indeed a book, - the most beautiful thing I've ever seen. It is far too heavy to conceal as one would a simple volume. Its weight is that of a child – it would need two men and a horse to steal and carry that any distance. We have heard of merchants from France in the guesten house, extra monks in the Abbey and we've found the clothes of the merchants, who are obviously sliding in and out of the Abbey – the regime there is so slack that they probably didn't need an accomplice, - just somebody local to ease their way– I begin to see the scene more clearly."

He turned his horse towards the Abbey.

"Good Friday or not, The Abbot must see us now."

Chapter 14

Surprisingly, Sir Tobias had no difficulty in gaining access to Abbot Bradford. The Abbot looked tired and dispirited, - not his usual arrogant self, for news of the discovery of the boy's body had reached him.

Sir Tobias told him details of the discovery of Roger's body and in what condition.

"He had been imprisoned in this room for at least two days I would surmise. His garments were much befouled with his own excrement, and he had been severely beaten more than once. How long had your order owned this property?"

"Nearly a year. It is our intention to expand the school house run by Thomas Copeland."

"Have you given any thought to your beautiful missal?"

"I believe it to be a thing of great beauty – unusually perfect, which sings the Glory of God." The Abbot sounded almost humble.

As he spoke, Prior Simon burst into the room with scarcely a knock.

"Father Abbot, - you must come – Oh, I beg your pardon, but the good Coroner may wish to see – the missal room is open – and"-

Prior Simon's incoherence caused all three men to rise to their feet. Abbot Bradford led the way down to a stone-flagged passage, and towards the room in which

Sir Tobias knew the missal was housed. There were two agitated monks guarding the door, and they stood aside as the Abbot approached. There was no need for a key – the door was already unlocked. The party stepped inside, where Prior Simon had stationed another monk to guard his prisoner. Matthias swept his eyes round the room and took in the scene. The missal was open; the glorious illustrations caught his eye at once; the luminosity shone on the pages – delicate lettering, careful line drawings and patient observation to detail glowed for all to see. He, a lover of books and learning in all its forms, caught his breath.

Abbot Bradford caught his breath for an entirely different reason. As he turned the intruder roughly to face him, it was none other than Father Samuel.

"*What* are you doing here?" he hissed.

Father Samuel's eyes were closed in prayer, and he did not reply. Sir Tobias closed the great door behind him.

"Father Samuel, - before the Abbot and before God, are you the killer of Roger, Mary's brother?" he asked, very directly and quietly.

Father Samuel's eyes jerked open and met Sir Tobias' eyes.

"No! Is the boy dead?" he gasped.

"Extremely." replied Matthias.

"Explain this intrusion!" spluttered Abbot Bradford.

Sir Tobias held up a hand for calm.

"This is much more serious than an intrusion," he said, "we most urgently need the full story in order to untangle the more sinister one."

Father Samuel cast a last, longing look at the perfect page in front of him, and drew from his pocket a key.

"I have sinned," he said, simply. "I fell on the slippery grass when helping Mistress Fosse away from the garden the day Mary died. I fell upon a key, and without knowing why I did so, I pocketed it. After a little investigation, I discovered that it was the key to this door – and its wondrous, joyful incredible missal.. which should surely be shared with all to see the Glory of God.."

The Abbot bristled. "*Preposterous idea!.*"

Sir Tobias interrupted him

"We are talking of three violent deaths, - not Abbey rights," he snapped.

Father Samuel continued, "I have used the key three times only – I am careful when I touch the pages and I always return it to the page of the day. – the beauty of it is magnificent. It was never difficult to slip into the Abbey unobserved , and I was never stopped

Abbot Bradford was silent. However much he disliked the little priest, his sincerity and appreciation of the work touched him just a little.

"Father Samuel, three people have been murdered for this key," Sir Tobias told him, soberly. "Is that really all you can tell me?"

The priest turned to face him.

"On my oath, that is all. I have slipped into the Abbey three times, each time during the evening. I have used the key, unobserved, three times and each time I have seen the missal in all its splendour. It is the most wonderful thing I have ever seen."

"Then if that is all, we now need to set a trap for the perpetrators of the intended theft," Sir Tobias decided.

"Theft?" Father Samuel said, startled. "Who would be able to steal this wondrous thing?"

"That is what you are going to help us discover," Sir Tobias told him grimly.

Abbot Bradford glared at him.

"How could a priest of my choosing *dare* to use a key and...." Sir Tobias stopped him with a frozen look.

"If we can use Father Samuel to catch a three times murderer, and two merchants masquerading as monks within your community-"

Abbot Bradford's jaw dropped.

"I have no monks masquerading-" he began.

"How many monks do you have?" Matthias asked him softly.

"Twenty four" he replied.

"There were twenty six in your procession this morning," Matthias told him. "I counted them myself."

The Abbot was silenced.

"If Father Samuel can help us to set a trap for these false monks, and even lead us to their master, if indeed there is one, then I am sure his iniquities will be forgiven," Sir Tobias said.

Father Abbot and Prior Simon glanced at one another.

They knew they had no choice.

Father Samuel of All Hallows left the Abbey some time during the afternoon of Good Friday. He had business of his own to attend to leading up to Easter Sunday, but he had temporarily lost his zest for a fight with Abbot Bradford. He deemed it wise to postpone that for a few months. Before Father Samuel left the shelter of the Abbey, Prior Simon let it be known to one or two carefully chosen monks of a more garrulous nature that someone had a key to the missal room. Father Samuel had no idea as he left, whether he was being followed or not.

As Sir Tobias had directed , he mentioned the discovery of the key and the sightings he had enjoyed of the missal to anyone he met – parishioners, fellow priests, - and he made no attempt to keep his voice down. As he reached his own small home, a cold shaft of fear shot through him like an arrow. The bait was laid. Who would be the taker?

Easter Sunday passed without event. Father Samuel preached to his little flock – the processional squeezed through the narrow doorway to the baptisms, and if the flock were disappointed by Father Samuel's lack of action against the Abbot on this occasion they did not show it. Matthias and Sir Tobias tried to make themselves inconspicuous in the congregation, wary and watchful. Davy and William were elsewhere, armed, watching and waiting. Sir Tobias felt the end was near, and had despatched messengers to the Sheriff at Dorchester.

The priest from Oborne called on Matthias the Monday after Easter. He came to thank Matthias on behalf of Mary's family, and to inform him when Roger's burying was going to be, should Matthias wish to attend.

Before he left, he glanced anxiously at Matthias.

"Father Samuel's mission seems a very desperate one," he began, apologetically. "Is he to be protected in some way? I would not wish a further death."

Matthias hesitated. Father Samuel had clearly spread his story well.

"I think he will be well guarded," he replied, uncertain how much information he should impart.

"I would accompany him," the young priest said, earnestly. "It is not right for him to undertake this task alone."

Matthias thought for a moment. The plans laid by Sir Tobias were thorough and comprehensive, but to have a fellow priest accompany him as he walked to the Abbey would surely be an encouragement to Father Samuel.

"Father Samuel is not a fighting man – his physique is but willowy – you could be sending him to a senseless end," urged Father Peter.

Matthias looked squarely at him. Father Peter was young, strong, physically fit, - and he must have seen Roger's body and know the ruthless efficiency of the killer.

"Ride into Sherborne this evening," he decided, "if the Coroner sees fit, you shall accompany him to the Abbey"

Matthew watched him ride away, lost in thoughts that were not wholly easy., although he couldn't quite say why.

Each member of the party watched and waited. The appointed time came – and went. Of Father Samuel there was no sign. A doubt crept into Matthias' mind as he crouched among the scaffolding and debris outside the Abbey. Where was Father Samuel? He knew only too well the importance of luring the killer from the shadows and into the light. He had promised to be there – and he had Father Peter to accompany him, with the Coroner's blessing.

Cold horror suddenly clutched at Matthias' heart. He suddenly knew the truth. He had watched Father

Peter ride off – he couldn't place the feeling of unease then, but he could now.

He broke from his hiding place with a shout.

"Sir Tobias! To Father Samuel's house! Quickly!"

The urgency in his voice galvanized all into action. Footsteps pounded across the green and towards the bottom of Cheap Street where Father Samuel's house stood back to back with the bakehouse.

The front door stood open but no light came from within.

"Torches!" called Sir Tobias, and William pounded on the bakehouse door for some light.

By the flare in William's hand the circle of men could see Father Samuel's body, still bleeding, still twitching slightly. His throat had been cut with the same precision as Roger's. There were signs of a scuffle, but Father Samuel had been no match for his attacker.

"There should be two bodies," Davy said, breathing hard.

"No," Matthias answered, "One. The other is our murderer. I hope he hasn't got far."

Sir Tobias bent to touch Father Samuel. The body was still warm. He shouted instructions, and William mounted his horse and rode to the Castle for re-enforcements.

The Abbot's bailiff knelt by Father Samuel's still warm form.

"*Who* has done this?" he exclaimed, uncomprehending of Matthias' sudden understanding.

"The priest of Oborne," Matthias told the assembled party.

"He asked permission to accompany Father Samuel for safety – and we agreed. I thought it would offer some comfort to Father Samuel in his fear of his mission.

173

It was only when he failed to turn up that I realised that it was Father Peter's retreating horse and shape that were so familiar – I had seen them on the night of the fire, and again when he called at the house to speak to Davy. No wonder he knew how to find us."

"He'll be making for Poole," Sir Tobias realised.

The night became a blur after that.

Sir Tobias, William, Matthias and four mounted soldiers from the Castle set off for Oborne, but as Sir Tobias predicted, the priest-house was empty and dark. Father Peter had packed his belongings, and the place held no clue as to the when and why.

The sea captain from Poole would be ready to take them aboard – blood on their hands notwithstanding. Gold talks. Sir Tobias knew, and he had no doubt that the passengers were "they" and not just "he." The bogus monks had been the look-out men, the bully boys, and they too would be gone with Father Peter. The lax conditions pervading in the Abbey no doubt had allowed them to join the processing monks at will, and roam about the Abbey unchallenged, - unless there was an accomplice within – and Sir Tobias now rather doubted that.

The three travellers on the coast road were silent as they rode. Their horses were lathered and spent. When they spoke, it was in their native tongue –a French patois. They didn't need to glance behind them – they had ridden half the night and slept little in order to put distance between themselves and Sherborne, for this was a planned exit once they understood that the great missal was not to be theirs – yet.

But they had the key – that was proof for their master that they had not deceived him all these long months spent in this cursed country, - and it might still be of use to them in the future.

"The Duke will be displeased," the merchant said, between clenched teeth. The wind was stinging his eyes.

The priest shrugged his shoulders, straining his eyes for the first glimpse of the coast.

"We have achieved something – four dead Englishmen and knowledge of their great treasure. The Duke would have it in his own treasure-house."

"Three Englishmen and a maid," said the third traveller, quietly. He was younger, and less-used to such ruthless bloodshed.

The priest shrugged again.

"What matter?" he said, carelessly, "They are all English vermin."

The younger man folded his lips and said nothing. His bearded companion pointed forwards.

"Look! The coast! Pray God our sea-captain is this side of the narrow sea."

The priest nodded and spurred his horse on. His had been the hardest part of the task – leaving his mother-house to masquerade as an English priest, to search out the missal his master had heard of, and to set up his two companions to spy out its exact wherabouts and enlist local help.

They had thought themselves fortunate to find Roger, a willing thief. The young married man had not been so easy – he'd become greedy and nearly spoiled all the carefully laid plans – plans which had taken him two years. Two years in England he'd spent – building up contacts – living the life of a young and eager priest, when all around him were the hated English. His appointment to the living of Oborne had been the result of a year of waiting...waiting for the right opportunity, and he had worked so hard at appearing to be the perfect, courteous, compassionate village priest.

His father had been an English soldier, a deserter from the battlefields who'd lived a delicious life of sin with Pierre's mother – and taught the young boy his language, and Pierre, with his quick ear and talent for mimicry had put the skill to good use. His father had died from an arrow wound when the boy was fourteen – an English arrow – a fellow soldier had run him to earth and he'd paid the price for his desertion.

A life of prayer and devotion had followed, - but always the desire for revenge on the English. And so it had come – his opportunity – when the Duke had sought a man of God with command of the English tongue. The great and magnificent missal of Sherborne was his goal, and he'd laboured at the task for two weary years. So near were they to success that Pierre could almost weep at the missed opportunity, - but tomorrow was another day, and the bothers of Sherborne would not mend their ways for very long, he was sure. Their English arrogance would take care of that.

The town of Poole lay in front of them. Luck was on their side, although the unfriendly sea was tipped with angry foam

The sea-captain was in port – his vessel trimmed and ready. Gold passed hands for the last time.

By the time Sir Tobias and his party caught up with them, they would be half way to France.

Matthias stared in bleak and bitter disappointment at the departed vessel, now hardly visible on the churning grey sea.

Visions of Ben, of Mary, of Lydia's burning house and the dreadful fate of Roger and Father Samuel danced before his tired eyes. Sir Tobias, beside him, grunted in disbelief.

"We have no power over them now," he said, shaking his head.

"What of the sea-captain?" Matthias asked.

"He'll deny any knowledge of them, and in any case, he may well have been ignorant of their purpose and their deeds."

Matthias was unused to such hard riding. He ached from lack of sleep, and was still amazed and stunned by the ruthless killings he had experienced.

"How can a so-called man of God justify these actions?" he asked, hopelessly. He rubbed his eyes with his knuckles to hide the hot and childish tears that he could hardly restrain. The apparently senseless slaughter appalled him.

"We are still at war with France, Matthias," William reminded him. "Priest or not, we are still the enemy. Our Oborne priest came here with a mission – an order from high places, which was to snatch the missal from under our nose and to allow a French court or monastery of some standing to glory in the possession of it. They would not let English dogs stand in their way. The young priest must have had some English parentage for his command of our language to be so good – no trace of any misplaced vowels – but we can only guess at his side of the story."

"Abbot Bradford will learn to have some care over his missal now," Sir Tobias said, turning his horse towards the North. "We can do no more here. We cannot bring these men to justice – we can only bury our dead and look to the future."

The party spent that night in the monastery in Wimborne, and a little rested but very subdued, rode into Sherborne late on the second afternoon.

Sir Tobias spent some time closeted with Abbot Bradford, and then he and William and Matthias turned up Cheap Street to join the track which led to Milborne Port and Purse Caundle.

"My judgement was flawed in several places," Matthias admitted, wryly, before they parted.

"You only do what you think is right at the time," Sir Tobias assured him. "I agreed that Father Peter should go to Father Samuel. We had no idea of his real purpose. You believed a man of God to be just that – a man of God, not a ruthless killer acting for French duke or bishop, with an eye on the main prize. Concentrate now on your schooling, Matthias, and learn from this episode of the corruption war and greed brings to the human heart."

He raised a hand in farewell as Matthias turned off the track and trotted towards the church. Matthias turned back one last time before reaching his home. Sir Tobias and William were watching him home...almost father figures, thought Matthias.

"Come and see us often, Matthias!" called Sir Tobias, as he and William spurred their mounts into action again.

Davy and Elizabeth were waiting by the gate when they had heard the horses' hooves. Elizabeth looked older and more careworn, and there was still the glass by the front door to replace.

Davy reached up his hand and took the bridle and Matthias dismounted painfully. He tried not to hobble as he entered his own house again, but his legs would hardly hold him.

"I'm not a long distance rider, Davy," he said, sinking onto the settle where Elizabeth had put cushions. "I don't think I'll be able to rise from here for several days!"

Davy laughed shakily – he had been afraid he might not see his master again.

"The day after tomorrow we expect your first batch of pupils," Davy said, "So there's much to be done in a day.

Matthias looked round his home, and fleetingly, his mind lingered on Lady Bridget's tasteful furnishings, and wondered what Alice's home looked like, - and then he set his mind resolutely to his own future. In a day, his new life as a schoolmaster would begin – he would need to be ready for them.

The Author's Notes

The difficult years of Henry VI's reign caused unrest and turmoil, culminating in what we know as the wars of the Roses.

Sherborne, in Dorset, had unrest of its own during this period of history, as Abbot Bradford had made alterations to All Hallows' church, adjoining the Abbey, which enraged the townspeople.

Abbot Bradford was Abbot of Sherborne....and he was, in character, as described in this novel. The schoolmaster, Thomas Cope, was also a real person, and it is thought that one of the misericords in the Abbey, which show a schoolmaster beating a boy, may well have been Thomas Cope. You can see this under one of the choir stalls.

Bishop Neville was Bishop of Salisbury at this time, and the actions taken by him described in the book are factual.

The story of the attempted theft of the Sherborne Missal is fictional, although it disappeared at the time of the dissolution of the monasteries, resurfaced at the time of the restoration and was later discovered in France, mysteriously, in the hands of the Bishop of Lisieux. How he came by it is not recorded. After passing through the hands of several dedicated book collectors in France, it was purchased in 1797 by George Galway Mills. From there it went to Hugh,

Duke of Northumberland for the sum of £215 and remained in the hands of the dukes of Northumberland for 200 years, before being generously loaned indefinitely to the British library in 1983.

More information on the ownership of this valuable manuscript can be obtained by reading The Sherborne Missal, by Janet Backhouse.